Benjamin Leopold Farjeon

The March of Fate

A Novel: Vol. II.

Benjamin Leopold Farjeon

The March of Fate
A Novel: Vol. II.

ISBN/EAN: 9783337031879

Printed in Europe, USA, Canada, Australia, Japan

Cover: Foto ©Andreas Hilbeck / pixelio.de

More available books at **www.hansebooks.com**

THE MARCH OF FATE.

THE MARCH OF FATE.

A Novel.

BY

B. L. FARJEON,

AUTHOR OF

"GREAT PORTER SQUARE," "TOILERS OF BABYLON,"
"A YOUNG GIRL'S LIFE," "THE MYSTERY OF M. FELIX," &c.

IN THREE VOLUMES.

VOL. II.

LONDON :
F. V. WHITE & CO.,
31, SOUTHAMPTON STREET, STRAND, W.C.
1893.

PRINTED BY
KELLY AND CO. LIMITED, GATE STREET, LINCOLN'S INN FIELDS, W.C.,
AND KINGSTON-ON-THAMES.

CONTENTS.

The Third Link—Fashioned of Letters Written by Lovers and Friends, False and True.

THE MARCH OF FATE.

THE MARCH OF FATE.

• —

The Second Link—Supplied by Mr. Barlow, Private Inquiry, Surrey Street, W.C.

— ◆ —

CHAPTER XVII. *(continued)*.

THE DIARY CONTINUED.

WHETHER months or years have passed I cannot say. I boasted of my memory once; it has failed me, and I can no longer depend upon it.

I have been haunted by visions and terrible images and fancies. I cannot separate the real from the unreal. I know not what is false and what is true. Here in my loneliness I sit and write, and what I write shall go to her to whom I pour out my soul. I will find a way. Have I not succeeded in stealing paper and pen and ink? In the midst of my delirium I have an occasional hour of reason, an hour in which I am able to think of the horrible past, to grope through fact and fancy. " Be calm, Adeline," I say to myself ; " be strong ; hold fast to the present ; brush aside the phantoms ; set the truth plainly before you."

I will do what I can. If I fail, forgive me, and out of the goodness of your heart unravel the mesh which bewilders me.

It is true that I live—it is the unhappy truth. I prove it. This sheet of paper is stained with my blood.

It did not hurt me. I can conquer physical pain, if I cannot conquer the phantoms which lurk in the air. I know they are there, though at this moment I behold them. I cannot because I will not. I could call them to my sight, but I hold them back till I have finished the task I have set myself. While I have a spark of reason left I will use it to tell my story to the end. Pity me, pity me !

Yes, it is true that I live. Feeble as I am, I still draw breath. The door is locked,

but I can see through the window. There
are trees with waving branches upon the land.
Birds flutter through them. The blue clouds
sail on. I am warm. It is summertime.
Summertime! Alas!

It is true I had a child, a baby girl, with
breath like the perfume of violets, shaming
mine. I held her in my arms; I kissed her
sweet mouth. She is gone; she is lost.
Dead, dead!

So they told me. I do not remember
when, but they told me. I am ready to
swear it. O, my baby, my sweet! Would
you have lived if I had been a better mother
to you? Is it I who worshipped you—is it I
who killed you? They did not say so!
" Murderess!" Other things as horrible have
been whispered to me, as horrible and as
false as this. It is done to madden me. I
have heard it said that I am mad. But do
mad people do what I am going to do now?

There was bread in the room. I broke
some into crumbs and put them out on the
window-sill. There were iron bars to the

windows, through which I could thrust my hand.

The birds came and flew away with the crumbs, and I did not stand far from them. Would they have done that if I had been mad?

And yet what I have heard them say is true, but not always true—not true at this moment; only they doubt whether I am ever sane.

This is not a prison; it is a private asylum for those who give way to their horrible craving for drink.

"Do you wish to get well?" It was a doctor, not the nurse who attended me in Paris, who asked the question. "Do you wish to live?"

"Yes," I answered.

"Sign this paper," he said, "and there is hope for you. Refuse, and you are lost."

"Why should I sign a paper?" I said. "You have done what you liked with me; you are doing what you like with me."

"What is being done," he said, "is for

your good. There are times when you are not accountable for your actions. You are an English subject, and you cannot be taken where you can be cured without your written consent."

"When I am well," I said, "shall I be set free?"

"You will," he replied. "For your own sake, for your child's sake, sign."

I put my name to the paper, which the doctor read first; but I did not hear what he said. My only thought was that I must try to get well for the sake of my child.

There is a noise in the passage without. Some one is coming in. I must hide this paper, and play the hypocrite.

The door is unlocked, and the master of the house enters. I do not know his name, and I have seen him only twice before. He reminded me then of a fox, and he reminds me of one now. He has a long, thin, pointed face, with cunning eyes, which say, "Do not trust me, do not trust me." He does not think that his eyes betray him.

I am on my guard. On the two previous occasions on which I saw him I was ill, and we held no conversation. He spoke only to a woman who attends to me, whom I address, as she bade me, as Gabrielle. She is quite a different person from the nurse who looked after me in Paris, and looks as if her life had been a life of trouble. I have asked her questions about myself, which she has evaded answering, not from unkindness, but from fear of the master.

"Pray do not press me," she said. "The master will come and see you one day, and then you can speak to him. But be careful what you say; he is very clever."

By clever she meant cunning, so when he enters my room now I set myself a task, to be as cunning as he is. There are a good many things I want to know about, and I do not see how I can get the information from any one but the master.

Gabrielle follows him into the room, and stands submissively at the door. The master holds out his hand, I place mine in it. He presses my fingers caressingly, insinuatingly, as though he would read my thoughts through them.

"You are better to-day," he says.

"I am well," I reply.

"No, no," he says, in gentle correction, "better, but not well."

"You know best," I say.

"Yes," he says, "I know best. Gabrielle says you wish to speak to me."

"I asked her to tell you so."

"I am here, you see," he says, almost gaily, "at your request. You are calm?"

"Quite calm."

"What we have to guard against," he says, his fox-like eyes fixed on my face, "is dissimulation, deceit, artfulness to gain the end a patient has in view. The practice of these deceptions is always followed by punishment. Is it not, Gabrielle?"

"Always, master," she answers.

"I am not clever enough to deceive you," I say, "and if I were there is nothing to be gained by it."

" That is well said."

He motions to Gabrielle to leave the room, and the master and I are alone.

" You wish to speak to me," he says ; " I also wish to speak to you. You wish to know something. Let me see if I can answer."

" How long ago is it since I was brought here ? " I ask.

" Eight months," he answers.

" Is it possible ? "

" It is better than possible ; it is true. The date of the entrance of every patient in this house is recorded in the books."

" I signed a paper, did I not ? "

" You did. Without your signature you could not have been admitted."

" Entering of my own free will, can I leave of my own free will ? "

" It will be prudent," he says, " not to immediately answer the question."

" You may answer it at another time ? "

" Perhaps at another time."

" You perceive that I am rational."

" Appearances are not to be trusted."

Desirous to avoid the least symptom of contention I pass from the subject.

" I had a child," I say, my voice trembling, my heart throbbing.

" I was so informed. You have lost her ? "

There was no compassion in his voice ; it was as cold as steel.

" It is really true ? " I ask, with difficulty controlling my voice.

" It is really true."

I do not speak for several minutes. I expected this confirmation, but could not bear it without deep suffering.

Having borne this ordeal, I could bear others.

" What malady was I suffering from when I was brought to this house ? "

" It is expressed in the document you signed."

" But let me hear my shame ! " I plead.

" As you will," says the master. " You had a craving for strong drink which was driving you mad. You came here to be cured."

"Am I cured?"

"I cannot say."

"Surely you are wise enough and clever enough to tell me! I implore you!"

"I will tell you to-morrow."

With this assurance I am forced to be content. To-morrow! It is only a few hours. And now for information upon a matter which has agitated my mind.

"This is a private establishment?" I ask. I know that it is so because Madame Gabrielle has told me, but the reason why I ask the master is that it leads naturally to what I wish to learn.

"It is."

"Kept up at your own expense?"

"Assuredly."

"You are a philanthropist?"

"Oh, no; I am a business man."

"But a philanthropist as well." He looks at me, and shrugs his shoulders. "It costs money being kept here?"

"Yes, it costs money."

"Who pays for me?"

"Ah," he says, repeating my question, "who pays for you?"

"Will you not tell me?"

"There are confidences," he replies. "Be content that you have friends."

"Friends?"

"One, at least."

A glance at his face assures me that it will be useless to press the inquiry, but with Clifford in my mind I venture to ask:

"Is he a gentleman?"

"Oh, yes, undoubtedly a gentleman, having money."

That is the test, in his view, and he states it with an indisputable air.

"Has he been to see me?" I ask.

"He has not."

"Where is he now?"

"I do not know."

"But he pays regularly, does he not, or you could not afford to keep me."

"He pays," says the master, "through a third party."

Then he puts an end to my questions by

saying, "I have been very indulgent. Ask nothing more to-day, but answer me."

He interrogates me as to who I am, whether I have parents, or brothers, or sisters living. Evidently he is curious about my history, and knows very little concerning it. I answer him truthfully up to a certain point, but I give him no clue of the one friend I have in America, and when he leaves me I see that he is dissatisfied, and that he believes I have been telling him untruths.

This that I have written must go to the post. Only Madame Gabriel can do it for me. It is strange that I have contrived through all my troubles and illness, to keep by me one five pound note, which I sewed in my dress when I was in Paris. Before Gabriel enters the room, after the departure of the master, I have picked the threads and extracted my treasure, but when she comes in I do not know how to commence. She assists me, however, by asking if the master had been kind to me, and I tell her what passed between us; and then I confess to her that I said nothing to him of the friend I have in a distant land.

"I have written to her," I say, "and there is no one but you who would post my letter to her."

She looks alarmed, but I appeal to her so successfully that she promises to do what I ask. I give her the five pound note, and she is to bring me the change for it, and some postage stamps. It is while she is gone that I am adding these lines.

If I am cured I shall surely be allowed to leave this place. The master will tell me to-morrow. But why could he not tell me to-day? Being well, they can have no excuse to detain me here. I will go and seek Clifford, but first I must see my child's grave.

Where have they buried her? I have seen pictures of spots where I should like her sweet body to rest, where I would like to rest myself. As I write, I can feel the tender clasp of her baby fingers, I can see her lovely eyes and face——

Hush, Adeline—be calm, do not give way. So much depends upon it. Your life, your liberty, your future. To be confined within these walls for ever would truly drive me mad. "A craving for strong drink which was driving you mad." The master's words. It was Clifford who led me to it. Upon his soul, as well as upon mine, lie the sin and the shame.

What is the meaning of the sudden thirst that steals upon me, that parches my throat, that causes my eyes to wander to every corner of the room? Am I cured? I shall know to-morrow. I am trembling in every limb. Gabrielle's step without. I must hide my writing—no, I am forgetting. She is to post it for me.

* * * * *

To-morrow has come and gone, and I know whether I am cured.

I had fallen asleep in my chair, and when I awoke no one was with me. There was a dim light burning, depending from the centre of the ceiling, where I could not reach it.

The parching of my throat continued, and I went to the table to get some drink. There was .a wooden cup there, an earthen water bottle, and another bottle. I took out the cork, and smelt it. I held the bottle in my shuddering hands, put it down—carefully, so that it should not be broken—and tottered back to my chair.

I can recall every thought, every little incident of those few conscious minutes. I covered my eyes with my hands, and struggled with the temptation. But my throat was burning, and a devil was whispering in my ear. "Don't be a fool," it said. "Open your eyes and look round the room. It resembles a tomb. Bring light and gladness into it, and to your heart as well. It is so simple! Just one little drop! Take it as a medicine—you need it. Why spend the night in wretchedness? Just one little drop!"

As a medicine, yes—and I do need it, sorely, sorely. Just one little drop—no more; and I would put water to it. Why, a doctor would give it to me! Where, then, was the harm of helping myself?

I rose, and stood by the table, the wooden cup in my hand. I poured some brandy into it, and added water; then, without pausing to think, drank it off.

In a moment everything was changed. Gloom fled from the room, from my heart. I laughed aloud. But I had taken so little! If those few drops had effected such a transformation, had made me strong and happy, and bright, how much would a little more do?

The second time I drank it without water, and then in wild and joyous excitement, I drank again and again, till not a drop was left. The bottle dropped from my hand, and rolled upon the floor. I tried to catch it, and in the attempt fell, and could not rise.

*   *   *   *   *

Four days ago I made up my mind to escape, but I could not have succeeded without the assistance of Gabrielle. She heard my story; she told me hers. It is the old story of betrayal and desertion. She was going to leave her service in a month she said, and she would risk being turned away before. I recompensed her by giving her twenty francs. I have very little money left now.

I could obtain no satisfaction from the master. I told him that I did not intend to stay any longer in his house, and he said he would think about it. Had my door been left open I should have walked out at once, but he kept it always locked, and he took care to have every movement I made watched. The bond of sympathy established between me and Gabrielle caused me to open my heart freely to her.

"Can he confine me here all my life?" I asked.

"I should say not," replied Gabrielle. "You are an English subject."

I thanked her for the hint, and two or three days afterwards I asked the master whether he had thought about my intention to leave his house.

"I have written about it," he answered.

"To whom?" I inquired.

"To the party who is responsible," he said.

"I am the only party responsible for my confinement in this prison," I said.

He interrupted me, saying it was not a prison.

"That is what I understood," I said. "I have done no wrong to anyone but myself, have committed no crime for which I am liable to the law. Give me the name of the responsible party, as you call him."

"That," said the master, "I decline to do."

"I will give it to you," I said. "His name is Clifford."

Fox as he was, I saw in his eyes that I was right, and I saw, also, that he was uneasy at the bold attitude I was taking. This made me bolder still.

"If he has authority over me," I continued, "he must be my husband. Has he informed you that he is?"

"I have asked him no questions," he said.

"Say that he is my husband," I pursued. "I am an English subject, and he cannot confine me here against my will. I revoke the document I signed, which I mistakenly signed. If you keep me imprisoned in your house, which you have told me is a private establishment, it is unlawful, and you can be punished for it."

"You can speak very freely," he said, "when you are in possession of your senses, but when you are not——"

"Even then," I said, "I am my own mistress, and not your prisoner. Am I free to go now?"

"I am afraid," he said, "that you must wait till I receive instructions."

"I will wait," I said, "but not for long."

A week passed, and still he paltered with me. Then I resolved to escape.

It was done in the night. I tore the sheets from my bed into strips, and tying them together, with Gabrielle's help, fastened them to the window sill. But I did not dare to descend to the ground by that means; I

17*

wished them to believe that I had escaped by the window. I went out through the door of my room and the street door, which Gabrielle unlocked and locked, and I stood, a free woman in an unknown land, surrounded by darkness.

I had received instructions from Gabrielle which I endeavoured to follow. Her sister lived a dozen miles away, and Gabrielle gave me a letter to her which would ensure for me food and shelter as long as I was able to pay for them. I was to follow the high road till it branched out left and right, and my directions from that point were sufficiently clear to lead me to the cottage. But in the dark I was too frightened to proceed, so I walked only a hundred yards or so, and waited for the sun. It was weary work, and I was not as strong as I thought. I had no alternative, however.

In the matter of money I had deceived Gabrielle, as I am deceiving everybody. My life, indeed, is now nothing but deceit. I told Gabrielle that when I was free I should

be able easily to obtain what money I required, and the simple soul believed me.
Perhaps that was the reason why she elected
to be my friend. I cannot say. There is
only one being in the world who is absolutely
truthful and good—the lady I once called
mother.

The first tinge of daylight showed me the
road, and I proceeded as quickly as my
numbed limbs would allow. I was fearful of
being pursued and caught, but I had resolved
to fight for my freedom with all my strength.
Nothing of the sort occurred. So far as I
knew I was not followed, nor was I molested
by any of the workpeople I met, though
many gazed in curiosity after me. My feet
were tender and my frame weak, and when
the full sun rose I was already exhausted. I
stopped at an inn and had something to eat
and drink, a dish of eggs and brown bread,
and two glasses of a kind of cherry brandy.
I would have drunk more, but I had strength
this time to resist the craving. Helpless,
I might fall into the toils again. I knew

it to be imperative that I should preserve my senses—that was my only reason for resisting.

Slowly I went on, and at nightfall was some distance from the cottage. At another cottage I succeeded in obtaining shelter; they had no bed to offer me, but they spread straw upon the earth which formed the flooring of their home, and there I lay till morning, paying them a trifle for the accommodation. At noon of the second day I reached the cottage where Gabrielle's sister lives. I presented Gabrielle's letter, and was warmly welcomed.

"You can have Gabrielle's little room," the woman said, "till she comes. She says she is coming soon. By that time you will want to go away."

I made a bargain with her for food and lodgment; so small was the sum she asked that I was able to pay her four weeks in advance, and still have a little money left. I would not rob the poor woman, though she would have trusted me. When the time came for payment my purse might be empty, so I secured her and myself for a month.

She took me to Gabrielle's room, and I helped her to set it straight; then I lay down on the straw mattress to rest. I slept, and in my sleep, as it seemed to me, I heard the voice of a woman speaking and singing to her babe. It is a sound there is no mistaking. The tears ran down my face; I put my hands to my eyes; my fingers were wet. I was awake, then; it was no dream, for I still heard the singing. I crept downstairs, and there was a baby in the woman's lap. I held out my trembling arms, and the mother smiled, and allowed me to take the child. She told me when her little girl was born. I do not know the date of the birth of my own darling, but it must have been at about the same time. Deep was my emotion as I nursed this little stranger, rocking to and fro, and trying to sing through my tears and anguish. The smiling face of the woman underwent a change; she regarded me seriously. Putting her hand on my arm, she said :

"You have been a mother?"

"A most unhappy mother," I said.

"And your child?"

I looked down upon the earth; then upward through the open cottage window.

"Poor child, poor child!" the woman murmured.

This note of sympathy was like the opening of heaven's gate to me. I had fallen very, very low; I was dishonoured, disgraced; and when the bitter truth was revealed to me, I had courted a deeper degradation, seeking only a selfish oblivion of my first disgrace. I was young; in the course of nature, if I preserved my health, if I did not ruin my constitution by degrading habits, there might be a long life before me. For the first time since the day on which Clifford had made his shameful, his infamous confession, I was inspired by a sentiment higher than mere selfishness and despair. I would try to be good; yes, I would strive to overcome the fatal infatuation which was destroying me, body and soul. It seemed to me as if the babe in my arms was a shield protecting me from all evil, enabling me to defy the demoniac temptation so often whispered in my ear. This helpless babe was all powerful in its holy influence. I would cling to it, and it should save me from the pit. I begged to be allowed to nurse the child when it did not need its mother, and the woman said, certainly, she would be glad, it would be a help to her. I thanked her, and that was the first night for many, many months on which I can say I was happy.

Two days have passed since then, and I feel that I am among friends. The husband is a labourer in the fields ; he goes out early and comes home late ; and the wife has to work hard too. They do not grumble at the toil ; they have just enough, no more, and they have been married only two years. It is yet the summer of love.

*   *   *   *   *

Whoever says there is hope for those who

have fallen, lies! Whoever preaches salvation for lost souls, lies! The happy hours were few. Night has come again.

It was a fête day. In great cities people go into the country for their holiday. They work in close streets and houses; fields and hedgerows are a paradise for them. But here on fête days they go to the wine-shops. What attraction can the fields they labour in from sunrise till sundown have for the toilers? None. Their paradise is the wine-shop.

So we all went: Gabrielle's sister, her husband and little Julie, their child.

There was a fair close by with more wine-shops, and there we went later in the day. People were drinking all around me, and I touched nothing but water. It sickened me; it made me faint; but still I resisted, growing weaker and weaker, while the craving grew stronger and stronger. The faces of my friends were flushed, even the mother's face as she tossed her baby in the air. In fear lest the little one should fall and be injured, I took it from the mother's arms. She laughed, and said :

" Yes, you are right. But it is only for to-day. To-morrow we shall be ourselves again. Don't be afraid. This is not the first time, and I hope it will not be the last."

These words had a singular effect upon me. " It is not the first time, and I hope it will not be the last." She had no fear of herself, for she said, " Don't be afraid;" and, " To-morrow we shall be ourselves again."

If they had such confidence in themselves, why not I? Surely I was as strong as they? " You are, you are," whispered the fiend. " Do not be shamed by them. You are town bred, educated, a lady; they are country clowns. See how merry they are. Follow their example and be happy."

I pressed my fingers to my ears; I talked louldly to little Julie, to drown the voice of the tempter; but it was like dust; it would not be denied. It whispered and whispered, drawing me on, maddening me. And still I resisted.

We entered a booth, but I did not see the entertainment. I wanted neither to see nor to hear; all I wanted was little Julie, my shield, close, close to my breast. The show was over; we trooped out.

"Come, Madame Straitlace," said little Julie's father, "it is your turn to treat now. Look at my pockets."

He turned them inside out; they were empty.

"Yes, it is your turn, your turn," laughed his wife.

I offered him a few small pieces of money, but he cried:

"No, no, I am not a beggar. We haven't come to that yet, wife?"

"No, indeed," said she.

"Show your friendliness," said the man, "and drink with us. It is the only way."

In jovial mood they dragged me to the wine-shop. Had the fiend whispered to me at that moment I should not have fallen again, but the voice was silent, the tempter being as conscious as I was myself of the

struggle going on within me. In desperation
I threw money on the counter, and taking
the glass Julie's father held towards me,
drained it in a moment.

" That's well done," said Julie's father,
" as well as I could have done it myself.
Your eyes are dancing in your head. It is as
it should be. This is not the time for long
faces. Here."

Another glass was held out to me, which I
drained like the first. The lights, the people
resembled fire-flies, flitting all ways at once.

"Where is my little Julie?" cried the man.
"Give me my little Julie."

He tried to take the child from my arms,
but I held it tight. We had a struggle, on
his side in fun and merriment, on mine more
seriously, and he obtained possession of Julie.
Thank God for that! She was not in my
arms during what followed.

Can I describe it? Suddenly, without
warning, the air was filled with cries of terror.
Some light material with which the wine shop
was decorated took fire, and in a moment the

place was in a blaze. The shrieking of women, the fighting for the doors, the beating down of the weak, the frenzied appeals and imprecations, were horrible. They ring in my ears now, those death shrieks; I see women in flames struggling and leaping. These live in my imagination; the reality was even more terrible. ·

The wine shop was burned to the ground, and some booths adjoining. The dead were carried out, and laid on the ground, their forms illumined by torches which men were holding. Among the dead were little Julie and her mother.

I fled. The forest was four miles from the spot, but I felt no fatigue till I reached it. There I sank upon the fallen leaves, and writhed in anguish. What hope was there in the world for me now? How I passed the night I know not. The sun rose upon a soul for ever lost. I cannot continue. . .

*   *   *   *   *

Once before, when I was wandering in darkness, did Mary Sternhold come to me.

I did not know then that it was she who called me sister, and would have wooed me to seek death in the quiet waters of the river. I know it now.

As on that occasion, there are shadows around and about me, dark shadows of despair, seeking rest. Will they ever find it? How long have they been wandering in their hopeless search? I ask the questions aloud? I am answered.

"They are not the same. Every day the sun sinks upon new recruits. The ranks are quickly filled."

" Who are you ? "

" Mary Sternhold. I came once before."

" I remember."

" It was before your baby was born."

" Alas, yes ! "

" Before your baby died."

" Do not torture me."

" I am here to bless, not to torture. I am here to give you peace."

" Have you found it yourself ? "

" I have, and I bring it to others who fear

the ordeal. Since I last spoke to you has happiness been your portion?"

"Black misery has been my portion."

"Why, then, do you tarry? The sweetness of the world is not for such as you. It is folly to continue to suffer, when you have the remedy in your hands. Your youth is blighted; you will be old soon—long before your time—and you will sigh in vain for the blessing that now may be yours. You have sinned unconsciously. Beware lest you sin consciously. Look at me."

A star fell, and in the swift transient gleam I saw the form of Mary Sternhold. It was clad in white. Peace shone upon her brow.

"Look upon yourself."

Again a star fell, and I saw my form for one brief moment, a form to shudder at, to fly from. Torn garments; a haggard face; dishevelled hair; eyes of wild despair.

"As you are, so should I have been, and worse, if I had cared to live. As you are, so should I have been, and worse, if I had refused the blessing I offer to you. Shall I show you what you will become if you are still obdurate?"

"No, no! I never heard of your end, Mary."

"Nor any one else. I took care of that. Only God saw."

"And was not angry?"

"You have seen me; you have seen yourself. Be persuaded."

"I am a coward. I not dare."

"Faint heart! There is one you do not think of."

"Who?"

"Your baby. She is waiting for you. She will open her little arms for your embrace. She will hold up her sweet face for your kiss. You can meet her now, but not in the time to come. Low as you have sunk, the worst has not befallen; you may not escape from it if you live."

I held my breath. The river was singing its lullaby of peace, of love, of release from wretchedness and despair. Led by the spirit of Mary Sternhold I walked slowly on. The branches were bending, there was a soft rustle of leaves, the air was charged with sobs.

"You are sure God will not be angry?"

"He will be pleased with you."

"And my baby will welcome me?"

"With gladness."

The water was before me. I raised my eyes to Heaven. Of that sad night I remember nothing more. . . .

       *   *   *   *   *

CHAPTER XVIII

FURTHER LINKS.

"This," said Mr. Barlow, "is the last communication — the scraps cannot be called letters—Mrs. Kennedy received in the handwriting of Adeline Ducroz. Whether they were all that were written is hardly likely, considering the circumstances and the many years that have passed, to be ever known. My own opinion is that many must have miscarried—for this reason : nearly all that I have read was written at lucid intervals. There were periods, long or short, when the poor girl was not accountable for her actions, and during those periods I have no doubt she scribbled sometimes in secret. I would give something out of my own pocket to get hold of these portions of her confession which never reached their destination."

"For literary purposes?" I asked, and

18*

as I put the question a suspicion crossed my mind.

"Yes," said Mr. Barlow, complacently, "for literary purposes."

"Look here, Barlow," I said, giving utterance to my suspicion, "these papers are genuine, I suppose?"

"What do you think?" asked Mr. Barlow in return, with an amused expression on his shrewd face.

"They are so extraordinary and unusual," I stammered——

"Go on, Millington," said Mr. Barlow. "What are you stopping for? Say what is in your mind. They are so extraordinary and unusual,"

"And in some parts," I continued, rather embarrassed, "although I am not much of a judge, so poetical——"

"Go on, Millington, go on," said Mr. Barlow, encouragingly, "and in some parts so poetical——"

"That I shouldn't be surprised to hear that you had made them up yourself."

"Much obliged to you for the compliment," said Mr. Barlow, "but your opinion of my powers is too high; it really is, Millington. If I were equal to such flights of the imagination I would throw up business to-morrow, and start my literary career at once. The papers are genuine—one of the strangest chapters in real life I ever met with. What you say about their being poetical here and there is true; I was struck with it myself. It only shows what may be hidden in a person which, but for some crisis, might never come out. They say poets are mad; here is a proof of it. Now let us carry the story on."

He tied the papers carefully together, having previously re-arranged them, put them aside and resumed:

"The receipt of these communications occasioned Mrs. Kennedy the greatest anxiety, but she had other anxieties of a strictly personal nature which prevented her from moving in the matter, even if she had possessed the means to do so, which she had not. At about that time her husband met with an accident which crippled him for life. She had not only to nurse him, but to attend to his business affairs, which otherwise would have fallen into ruinous confusion. Occupation enough for one woman. Her husband became a confirmed invalid, and for many years was confined to the house. Her first duty lay in their home, and she performed it bravely. The communications she had received from Adeline Ducroz ceased at a critical moment in the young girl's life. There is no room to doubt that, urged to the deed by a disordered imagination and by the desperate position to which she was driven, she attempted to commit suicide. How she was rescued, and what was her subsequent fate remained a mystery for several years, and when Mrs. Kennedy obtained a clue it was by one of those singular chances which I believe to be sufficiently common, though most people regard them as inexplicable and extraordinary. Some, indeed, go so far as to declare them to be direct acts of Providence, which, between you and me, Millington, is

sheer nonsense. Mr. Kennedy became so
confirmed a hypochondriac that it was necessary he should have some one continually
with him. 'It is impossible for you to attend
to him yourself,' said the doctor; 'you must
get a trained nurse.' And although Mrs.
Kennedy was at first reluctant to give her
husband into the care of a stranger she was
compelled eventually to take the doctor's
advice. She asked him to obtain a kind and
experienced person for the duty, and in the
course of a few days he sent her a French-
woman who could speak English well, and
whose certificates and letters of recommenda-
tion were unexceptionable. The engagement
was made, and, as you will see, led to an important result, apart from the service she was
hired to perform."

"This woman," I said, "represents the
singular chance you spoke of?"

"She does," replied Mr. Barlow.

I jumped at a conclusion. "She was the
woman who acted as nurse to Adeline Ducroz
in Paris?"

"You have guessed it," said Mr. Barlow; "the identical woman. She was with Mrs. Kennedy a couple of months before the discovery was made. Mr. Kennedy's condition became so bad that he could not sleep, and opiates had to be administered to him. This sometimes sets the nurse free of an evening, at which times she and Mrs. Kennedy would keep each other company. Her name was Madame Pau. One night, when Mr. Kennedy was asleep, Madame Pau commenced to relate some of her professional experiences in Paris and elsewhere, mentioning no names. She had nursed all kinds of patients, and her anecdotal reminiscences were drawn principally from the humourous side of her occupation. Suddenly an idea occurred to Mrs. Kennedy. ' Were you in Paris in 1867 ? ' she asked. 'And in 1868 as well, Madame,' replied Madame Pau. ' Following your occupation ? ' ' Yes, Madame.' ' At an institution ? ' ' No, Madame. I nursed patients at their private residences.' ' Is it possible,' thought Mrs. Kennedy, ' that this can be the woman who nursed Adeline ?' She asked the question boldly, and according to her account, the woman at first rather hesitated to reply. This hesitation strengthened Mrs. Kennedy's idea. She represented to the woman that she was deeply interested in the young lady to whom she referred, and after a little persuasion and the promise of a bribe, Madame Pau spoke freely. She had nursed Adeline Decroz, and she knew more than Mrs. Kennedy suspected. What she subsequently revealed is set down in narrative form by Madame Pau, in French, and afterwards translated by Mrs. Kennedy. Here is the translation, in Mrs. Kennedy's writing. You will find it interesting. It opens up a new field of speculation, and throws a light upon Mr. Julius Clifford's character."

Selecting a paper from the documents near him Mr. Barlow proceeded to read :

The statement of Madame Pau, late of Paris, now of the United States of America, relating to the case of Madame Adeline Ducroz:

I am not good at dates. Years I remember, but not months, or weeks, or days. It was in the year 1867 that I was engaged to nurse an English lady in Paris, Madame Adeline Ducroz, who was afflicted with the vice of many English ladies, a passion for drinking too much. Not wine. Spirits. I have nursed other patients, suffering from the same malady, and all of them, I am delighted to say, foreigners.

Madame Ducroz expected to become a mother, which was bad for her and for the unborn child.

I am not good at names, as well as dates; I have had to do with so many. But I remember, in Paris, two names in this case. One is the name of the patient, Madame Ducroz, the other is the name of her gentleman friend, M. Julius Clifford. He was a compatriot of the lady, like her an English subject.

She was an encumbrance to him. He told me she followed him about, and would not leave him. He was the victim, not she. But he wished to be kind to her—O, yes, he wished her to be happy. Not with him, with some one else.

"She is unreasonable," he said to me. "She is violent. She lies when she speaks. She is under the delusion that I promised to marry her. It is too ridiculous. I am a gentleman, and she has only herself to blame."

I asked no questions. It was not for me to do so. It was for me to perform the duties for which I was engaged. I performed them faithfully, and carried out my instructions.

For instance :

"She can have whatever she asks for. She loves to drink. Indulge her. Here is money! "

He was generous, M. Clifford, and rich. I performed my duties, but it did not belong to them to make her mad. She implored for drink. I would not give it to her, only a little by the doctor's instructions. It was the doctor's instructions I carried out. I forget the doctor's name.

It is not for me to declare whether the gentleman spoke true or false in what he told me about his lady. I have my ideas, that is all.

No, I would not give her brandy. She produced money, and said:

"Madame Pau, Madame Pau, I am perishing, I am dying! Bring me one little bottle!"

I refused. I would not.

But there were others about her who did what I refused to do. Patients suffering from Madame Pau's malady are very cunning. She bribed servants to get her what she wanted, and I found the empty bottles about the room. She drank herself delirious. It was deplorable to see her. It made me weep.

I spoke to her like a mother; I advised her for her good; she made promises; she did not keep them. It is a mania ; they have not the strength to resist.

I informed M. Clifford. He said :

"What can I do? She is not to be depended upon for one moment, not for one single moment. She deceives you as she deceived me. She is headstrong, she is ungovernable. It shall not be said I am not kind to her. Let her have all she wants."

I suggested that he should see and remonstrate with her. He would not. He had done with her, he said. So much money he would spend upon her ; then he would shake himself free.

He did not remain in Paris all the time. He went to England. And came back again. This happened three, four times. Once he said to me, with an air of gloom.

"All this trouble would be over if she were not to recover."

The sentiment was disagreeable to me; I expressed myself. He replied,

"Can I help it if she is well or ill? It is in her own hands."

A child was born, a beautiful little girl. Madame Ducroz wept over her, caressed her, adored her. Sometimes she said,

"She is my guardian angel!" Sometimes, "She is my curse!"

All this time we did not know whether she would get well or die. She had great strength, or she could not have lasted so long. To-day the doctor said one thing, to-morrow he said another. The child, too. Now she was well, now she was ill. M. Clifford made inquiries about her.

"She is beautiful," I said. "She is adorable. Will you not come and see her?"

No, he would not, nor would he permit me to bring the infant to him. It came into my mind, "Has M. Clifford a heart?"

The child sickened; there was danger. Madame Ducroz was alarmed. She allowed herself to be persuaded. For the child's sake she would place herself in the care of a skilful man who kept an establishment for the cure of such as she. She signed a paper and was taken away.

M. Clifford paid all the charges. If he did not have a heart, he had a purse. He dismissed me, and paid me liberally.

"Have I not done everything in my power?" he asked.

"Everything, monsieur," I said.

"Could any gentleman have done more?" he asked.

"No, monsieur, no," I said.

"Speak always well of me," he said.

But I speak as I feel. From a little child I spoke always the truth. It is not always wise, I know it, but when one has a conscience one does not stop to consider.

It is your wish that I should say something of Madame Ducroz' nature. There was good in it, much good, but she had no control. She was affectionate, she was passionate. She spoke softly, she spoke loudly. She could caress, she could scratch. Am I condemning her? No, a thousand times no. Women are not little kittens. They have reason, they have sensibility, they have feelings. Do all gentlemen think so? No. They do us not justice; but they are stronger than we.

M. Clifford told me one story; Madame Ducroz told me another. Which was I to believe? Or, was it necessary for me to believe one or the other? I was not their judge; I was a nurse engaged for certain duties; but both showed anxiety that I should pronounce judgment. It was not for me, no, it was not for me. To myself I said, " It is not a new story. It will end like the others. M. Clifford will go back to society, Madame Ducroz will go back to society. They will meet and shrug their shoulders, or laugh in each other's face. There is a song; ' We loved, we parted. You were all to me, you are nothing to me.' " We Frenchwomen have sentiment, but some of us learn to know the world. It is seldom that Englishwomen do.

The judgment I formed of the end of the story was wrong. It was, after all, different from the others.

Madame Ducroz had feelings. They were

outraged. She said to M. Clifford, before I was engaged to attend her, that she would be revenged, that she would revenge herself. She repeated this in her delirium. That was his fear. M. Clifford was very proud, and he was a coward. I do not blame him. I do not blame her. It is well that some false lovers should be made to shake in their shoes, should be made to suffer. When a woman takes the law in her own hands, it is bad for the man. M. Clifford knew this. He had read our newspapers, and Madame Ducroz not being a little kitten, he was afraid of her.

I bade M. Clifford adieu, and I saw him no more for three years. I will not be exact; it may be more, it may be less. I have only my memory, and it is not always good. But three years will do.

I met him in Paris. He looked at me, colored, and went on. My way was his; I followed him because of that. I could not help thinking of Madame Ducroz.

He turned, fixed his eyes upon me, drew himself up proudly.

"Why do you follow me?" he asked.

"Monsieur is mistaken," I said. "It is the road I am going."

He did not believe me. There are gentlemen who tell you so without speaking, who are suspicious of everything and everybody. M. Clifford is one.

"Say what you have to say," he said, "and begone." But though he spoke haughtily he took out his purse. He was more eloquent and gracious with his money than with his tongue.

"As monsieur permits me to speak," I said, "I may be allowed to inquire after the welfare of Madame Ducroz."

"She is dead," he said.

"Alas!" I cried. "Poor lady, to die so young!"

"Do not make me a scene in the street," he said, and he looked around in fear that anybody should hear, and put some money into my hand.

"And the child, monsieur?" I asked, after I had thanked him. "The sweet infant?"

"Is dead," he replied. "That is all you want to know?"

"It is all, monsieur," I said.

"Oblige me," he said, "if you meet me again, in Paris or elsewhere, by regarding me as a stranger. You have been paid for the services you rendered."

He called a carriage, and drove away.

"Monsieur Clifford," I thought, as I walked on, "is out of his trouble. What he wished for has happened."

It made me sad, the end of Madame Ducroz and her sweet child, both so beautiful and unfortunate.

It was perhaps one year, it was perhaps two years after this meeting with M. Clifford in the streets of Paris that I was engaged as nurse in the south of France. It was a hard case. For two months I was confined to the house, day and night, and when my service was terminated I gave myself a holiday before returning to Paris. I travelled and enjoyed myself, having saved a little money.

I arrived at a town near the sea. The day

19*

was Sunday, and all the people were in the sunshine, and again in the evening when the stars were out. A poor woman, almost in rags, passed me, walking unsteadily. I just saw her face, and I ran after her in amazement. Was it the ghost of Madame Ducroz I had seen?

I seized her arm; I looked at her more closely. She moaned.

"Let me go. I have done no harm?"

I should have doubted my senses if I had not heard her voice. Even then I could not be sure. Had not M. Clifford told me that Madame Ducroz was dead? Wherefore the lie if this poor woman writhing in my arms was she?

Her face was changed, but still beautiful. I describe her rags, her condition in one word—destitution. But still another word—misery.

"Madame Ducroz!" I said to her, in a low voice.

She looked at me, trembled, and made no resistance.

Again I said, "Madame Ducroz!"

All she said was, "It is my name. Be satisfied, and let me go. I have done no harm!"

"Do you not remember me?" I said. "The woman who nursed you in Paris when your baby was born?"

"My baby!" she moaned. "I am seeking her. Do not detain me. I must find her, I must find her. Listen. You will hear her calling to me!"

I heard no voice. But I saw what filled my heart with pity. A poor crazed sister in want and misery. I slipped a franc into her hand. Her fingers tightened upon it. She laughed—the laugh of one who was not in her right mind.

Suddenly she cried, "Look behind you!"

I loosened my grasp, and looked as she bade me. In my amazement I thought a spirit might be standing at my elbow, but I was startled by no such vision. Turning to Madame Ducroz, I found she had vanished. She had tricked me to escape.

A shadow could not have glided away more noiselessly.

I sought her till near midnight, but saw nothing of her. I asked questions of people who could not give me satisfactory answers. Had it not been that I held her in my arms and my franc was gone, I should have believed that I was dreaming. But it was not a dream; I am ready to swear it. I never saw Madame Ducroz again, nor have I heard anything of her. This is a true statement.

(Signed) MATHILDE PAU.

CHAPTER XIX.

THE PORTRAIT.

"MADAME PAU," said Mr. Barlow, "took genuine pleasure in putting her statement in dramatic form, after the fashion of her countrywomen. That, however, is not the cause of part of her statement being false and part of it true. Her desire was to place herself in an entirely favourable light. As to her description of her treatment of Adeline Ducroz in Paris she has been very careful to wash herself white. The truth of those wretched weeks is told in the communications to Mrs. Kennedy received from Miss Ducroz. Mrs Kennedy believes this; so do I. There is a serious discrepancy in the two versions, and it is this that leads me to doubt Madame Pau's veracity when she speaks of the conversations between her and Mr. Clifford. Sifting the statement carefully, I come to these conclusions. Madame Pau being nurse to Miss Ducroz: true. Her refusal to obtain drink for her patient: false. Her conversations and interviews with Mr. Clifford during the time she was nursing Miss Ducroz: highly coloured, or entirely false. Her meeting Mr. Clifford accidentally in Paris some three years afterwards: true. Her meeting Miss Ducroz in the South of France a year or two after that: true in the main. Her bestowal of charity: a fiction. The important feature in the statement is the establishment of the fact that Miss Ducroz was living some years after she ceased corresponding with Mrs. Kennedy, and there appears to be little doubt that she was living in misery and destitution. Now, it is my opinion, and Mrs. Kennedy is even stronger in this belief than myself, that the child—a girl, remember—also lived, and that the fiction of its being dead was invented for the purpose of putting an end to the trouble between Mr. Clifford and the poor lady he betrayed. Living, and acknowledged, she might have been used as a thorn in his side.

Much more convenient to have her taken away and brought up under another name, and after a time perhaps lost sight of altogether. I will finish with Mrs. Kennedy up to the period of her departure from the United States. The statement made by Madame Pau inspired Mrs. Kennedy with such distrust of the woman that she was seriously considering whether she should dispense with her services and obtain another nurse for her husband, when an event occurred which saved her the trouble of definite action. Mr. Kennedy died, and Mrs. Kennedy was alone. Reflection convinced her that it would serve no good end to make an enemy of Madame Pau, or to challenge her veracity. Far better to part friends. If she had concealed or injuriously misrepresented anything, the truth, supposing it could not be established by other means, might, through her cupidity, be extracted from her in the future; for almost immediately upon her husband's death Mrs. Kennedy had resolved upon a certain course of action. She was comparatively a rich woman; her husband's property had increased greatly in value, and advantageous offers were made to her for its purchase. There was nothing to detain her in America ; the lonely life before her was not a tempting prospect ; and what she had learned from Madame Pau revived her interest in her adopted daughter. She burnt with indignation against Mr. Clifford, and she was impressed with the conviction that both Adeline Ducroz and the child were still living. What more righteous task could she set herself than to come back to England, after the realization of her property, and endeavour to find them ? She had no object in life ; here was one to her hand ; and if, in the carrying of it out she could punish Mr. Clifford for the foul wrong he had perpetrated, all the greater would be her satisfaction. Now you know who my client is."

"Mrs. Kennedy herself," I said.

"Exactly. Mrs. Kennedy herself."

"Has she accomplished the first part of her task ? Is Miss Ducroz living, and has she discovered her ?"

"At the present moment," said Mr. Barlow, "I am not not at liberty to answer both of your questions. The first I can. Miss Ducroz lives."

"That will be news for Mr. Haldane. I suppose I may make use of it."

"I see no objection. And now, Millington, take this into consideration; you have been so interested in the unwinding of the story that I shouldn't wonder if it has escaped you. Miss Ducroz is in the land of the living, and also, for a certainty, Mr. Julius Clifford. That being the case, are they or are they not man and wife according to the law of this country?"

I gave a long, low whistle, and said, "It certainly escaped me."

"It opens up issues, you see. There may be grave consequences hanging to it. I have stated my opinion, that Mr. Haldane and Mr. Clifford are one and the same person. I want this proved, and proved soon."

"How can it be done?"

"It is a simple matter. Rachel Diprose,

your son's sweetheart, is Miss Haldane's confidential maid——"

"Good God!" I cried, starting up in
excitement at the mention of Miss Haldane's
name, and at the thought that she would be
involved in her father's exposure and disgrace.
That I should be instrumental in bringing
shame upon one so sweet and charitable presented itself to me as indescribably base and
treacherous. Then, there was my boy,
George. His happiness might be wrecked
through me, for Rachel Diprose would be sure
to take her young lady's side, and would look
upon me and all belonging to me with
abhorrence.

"Don't lose your head, Millington," said
Mr. Barlow. "I know what you're thinking
of, but you're wrong, my lad. Make up your
mind to more than one thing. First, that this
affair's got to be carried through. Second,
that I'd have carried it through to a certainty
if you hadn't been in it It might have taken
me a week longer, but that's the extent. Did
you ever know me beaten yet? Third, that

being in it, you can act the part of a friend to those you care for, and soften the blow that's got to fall on tender shoulders. I'm talking sense, Millington, my lad. If I hadn't taken on my commission, and you hadn't taken on yours, they'd have drifted into worse hands than ours. And we can always throw up if we want to ; but it won't be so good for the other parties—remember that. Now are you steady ? Shall I go on ? "

" Yes," I said.

" Right you are. To commence again. Rachel Diprose, your son's sweetheart, is Miss Haldane's confidential maid. It's ten to one she's got an album, and it's longer odds that there's a portrait of George in it, and two or three of herself, and portraits of lots of her relations, near and distant, from babies in little skirts holding on to their fat little toes to grandfather and grandmother, who'd like to be their own grand-children and commence life all over again. I want the loan of that album for just one day. You write to her for it, and say you're going to send her in its place a spick and span new one, with gilt edges, bound in morocco, to commence housekeeping with. She'll pack it up instanter, and you'll receive it by the following post."

"What will you do with it when you've got it?"

"That's my business, and it's my business to give it you back the day after you hand it to me, without a picture missing, and in company of the spick and span new album I've spoken of. Will you do as much for me?"

"Yes, I will," I replied.

"Write to-night," said Mr. Barlow. "Instead of returning the album through the post you can take it back when you go to Chudleigh Park to give Mr. Haldane some information about Adeline Ducroz that will interest him. I should advise you to wait three or four days before you do this; it will be time enough. I made a remark to you last night about Miss Haldane's age. Eighteen, you said?"

" I asked George this morning, and he said that is her age. He knows it through his sweetheart."

"That," remarked Mr. Barlow, "would be the age of Adeline Ducroz's daughter if she were alive this day. Upon your next visit to Chudleigh Park you might have a chat with some of the villagers, and learn from them when Mrs. Haldane was married, and how long ago it is since she died. They are sure to know all about a domestic affair of that kind." Mr. Barlow looked at his watch. " It's past six. Come home with me and have a cup of tea. Mrs. Barlow will be glad to see you. George won't expect you home before eight, and you can get back by that time."

George opened the door for me in his shirt sleeves. That son of mine never had an idle hour. He had turned a room in the house into a workshop, and there, when he had nothing else to claim his attention, he was always to be found, making all sorts of things for future housekeeping with which he

intended one day to surprise his Rachel. He
had just put the finishing touches to a work-
table for his little wife that was to be, with
drawers and flaps, and receptables for everything a woman needed in the way of needle-
work. I don't know how many weeks he
had been employed upon this table in his
leisure time, and it was a pleasure to see the
pride he took in it, and to see him handle it
as if it were a living thing, with sense and
feeling. In his workshop were a number of
other useful and ornamental articles, brackets,
small cupboards to hang on the walls, a
corner cabinet, fitted with glass and shelves,
and I don't know what all.

"It's the next best thing to having Rachel
with me," he said, "working for her and
thinking of her. Have you heard any news
of that Honoria girl?"

"None, George."

He laughed when I told him I was going to
write to Rachel to send me her album, and
that Mr. Barlow intended to present her with
a new one.

"She'll wonder what you want it for," he said. "The new one will come in handy for the house. Every little helps."

In due time the album arrived, with a pretty note from Rachel, saying she supposed I wanted to make the acquaintance of all her relations before she and George came together. She enclosed a list of the portraits, with the family names and ages, nephews, nieces, aunts and uncles, and grandmothers and grandfathers, just as Mr. Barlow had said there would be.

"Take the greatest care of it," said Rachel in her note. "There are portraits in it I wouldn't lose for the world."

"That is one of them," said George, as we looked at the portrait of Rachel's young mistress. "Next to Rachel's it is the sweetest face I have ever seen."

CHAPTER XX.

I GAVE the album to Mr. Barlow, and the following day he returned it to me in company with a new album, much handsomer than I expected he would purchase, requesting me to forward it on to Rachel Diprose, with all kinds of good wishes and a hope that he would soon have the pleasure of making her acquaintance."

"As I have obliged you, Barlow," I said, "perhaps you will oblige me now by telling me what you wanted the album for."

He cocked his eye at me knowingly. "You don't mean to say you don't know, Millington?"

"I don't," I replied.

"You've grown stale," he said, "out of training. Well, you're none the worse for it.

When I asked for the loan of this album I guessed that there would be other portraits in it than the portraits of pretty Rachel's relations. As a confidential servant she would be presented, from time to time, with portraits of her fellow-servants at the hall, and very likely, as a mark of approval, with the likenesses of the family she is living with. Such as the likeness of Miss Haldane, whose Christian name you said was——"

" Agnes."

" Exactly. Agnes. This is the young lady, isn't it?"

" Yes, that is Miss Haldane's portrait."

" To judge by her looks, a born lady. But looks are deceptive. Then I reckoned upon finding the likeness of Mr. Haldane, and here it is, if I don't mistake."

I had not given him the list which Rachel had sent me; he had to guess at the pictures and had done so correctly.

" That is Mr. Haldane's portrait," I said.

" After we joined forces, Millington," continued Mr. Barlow, " there seemed to me to be one point it was necessary to establish

20*

beyond doubt, and that was whether Mr.
Haldane and Mr. Julius Clifford were one and
the same person. I had my suspicions, and I
made no secret of them to you, but said I
to myself, 'Best make sure, Barlow.' So
I carefully removed from the album the
likenesses of Mr. and Miss Haldane, and
mixing them up with a hundred others, took
them to my client in a loose heap. 'Look
through these likenesses,' I said to her, ' and
see if there is anybody you know among
them.'"

I interrupted Mr. Barlow by asking whether
he thought it was quite fair to use Rachel's
album for such a purpose, and whether it was
not very much like setting a trap for the girl
—making her, as it were, an accomplice with
us against the family she was serving?

"Don't worry about that," he said.
"Rachel will never know anything about it
unless you tell her. In my opinion it is quite
fair; and as to setting a trap for her, that is
all nonsense. I provided a safeguard. My

client was about to look through the likenesses when I laid my hand on them. 'I am compelled,' I said to her, 'to make one stipulation. Some of these likenesses don't belong to me, and have been lent to me by a person you are not acquainted with. You must promise if you recognize any of them not to ask me where I obtained them.' Does that satisfy you, Millington ? "

"I suppose it must," I replied, "the mischief being done."

To speak the honest truth, I was in a nervous state to hear the end of his manœuvre.

"My client gave me the promise, and then proceeded to examine the pictures. She tossed one after another aside, came to the likeness of Mr. Haldane, and stopped. She changed colour, and in other ways was visibly agitated. 'When and where was this likeness taken?' she asked. 'I don't know,' I answered, and I told her there and then that I was not at liberty to answer any questions concerning it.

'But,' said she, 'you are acting as my paid
agent to discover Mr. Julius Clifford for me.'
I admitted it. 'This,' she said, pointing
to Mr. Haldane's likeness, 'is the likeness of
the villain we are searching for.' 'Oblige
me,' I said, 'by looking through the other
pictures and telling me whether you recognize any one else.' She examined them
all carefully, paused half a moment when she
came to Miss Haldane's likeness, put it with
the others, and finished her task. Mr.
Haldane's likeness was the only one she
recognized. I pressed her closely about it,
and asked her if she was sure that she was
not mistaken. 'I will swear to the likeness,'
she said. I tied all the portraits together and
took possession of them. 'You must leave
the case entirely in my hands,' I said, 'if you
continue to employ me. You can see that
I have not been idle, and that I am making
progress, but as regards these portraits I am
not exactly a free agent.' She pressed me
then harder than I had pressed her, but I
stood my ground, and would give her no

further satisfacion, saying that she must trust me entirely, or not at all. After a long discussion she gave way, and said she hoped I would deal honestly by her. And that is how the matter stands at present. Beyond all doubt, Mr. Haldane is the man who betrayed Adeline Ducroz. The question is now, what are we going to do?"

I could not answer him; I had come to a knot, and could not untie it. When I joined forces with Mr. Barlow, I had no idea that it would lead so straight to what was now disclosed. Mr. Barlow's client hoped that he would deal honestly by her; Mr. Haldane hoped that I would deal honestly by him. When I undertook his commission, it was my intention to do so; otherwise I should have thrown it up without hesitation; but in the light of the strange disclosures that had been made, could I continue to do so? This was the perplexing phase of the matter which came slowly to my mind during the silence that ensued after Mr. Barlow's question.

"I wish to heaven," I said, fretfully

and impatiently, "that Mr. Haldane had never written to me to come to Chudleigh Park."

"What is done,' observed Mr. Barlow, with cheap wisdom, "can't be undone."

"Not much comfort in that," I said, not over amiably. I was vexed with myself, vexed with him, vexed with all the world. "Nor is it a very original remark."

"Admitted," said Mr. Barlow, whose self-possession seldom deserted him, "but it is not to be despised because of its want of originality. It is a rare gift, Millington, originality, and I don't lay claim to it. Things run pretty much in grooves, as at this very moment with you and me."

"Don't be mysterious, Barlow," I said, quite disposed to lash myself into conspicuous ill-humour. "Never in my life have I been mixed up in such an affair as this. Why on earth did I allow myself to be dragged into it? If it wasn't for George——"

"Exactly," said Mr. Barlow. "If it wasn't for George. It was in the first

instance your affection for that good fellow
that led you into it. But many a man starts
on a journey, and pulls up on the road,
resolving to turn back. I will explain what
I meant when I said that things with you and
me are running in the same groove. Neither
of us anticipated the discoveries that have
been made, and it is as clear to me as it is to
you that we cannot go on working together.
The interests involved are too conflicting.
Between your client and mine exists a deadly
enmity, and, as honest men, we cannot serve
them both. One of us must resign. Which
one ?"

I was immensely relieved; he had shown
me the way out of my difficulty. "Let it be
me," I said.

Mr. Barlow concurred. " I should have
suggested it if you hadn't. You see, old
friend, I took the business up because I
happen to be *in* the business ; you took it up
because you had a personal interest in it, the
sweethearting of George and Rachel. Go to
Chudleigh Park, and make Mr. Haldane ac-

quainted with what you know through me, of Adeline Ducroz. Say that you learnt the particulars through a third party, and if he presses you to name the third party put it on to me to answer him. You will have a difficult conversation with him, according to my reckoning; he will want to know more than you are warranted to disclose, but you will judge how far you ought to go in the way of satisfying him. How does this strike you ?"

"It is all right, and, Barlow, it is a wonderful relief to me. I am not fit for business any longer; I have grown too fond of my ease, of my idle life, of my pipe, and my birds, and my garden."

"Happy man!" said Mr. Barlow, contemplatively. "I look forward to the time when I shall enjoy the same, with the addition of pen, ink, and paper, to immortalize my name. Now go and get rid of your burden."

"There is just one thing I would ask," I said. "Although I have done with the

affair I cannot cease to have an interest in
it. Let me know from time to time how you
get along."

"In confidence," said Mr. Barlow, " I will
keep nothing from you. And if you find
Honoria I shall be glad if you will recipro-
cate."

"Confidence for confidence," I said, gaily ;
with the weight off my shoulders I really felt
quite young ; "every bit of information that
comes to me shall be at your disposal. Good
day, old fellow."

"Good day," said Mr. Barlow. "Love to
George and Rachel."

When I got into the streets, I walked along
briskly, humming a favourite air ; I seemed
to have got rid of the nightmare. My days
were once more my own, or would be after
my interview with Mr. John Haldane, for
whom, knowing him now to be Julius Clifford,
I would not have continued to work for any
consideration. But had it not been for the
prompt suggestion of Mr. Barlow, I might
have taken a longer time to make up my

mind. I was thankful indeed that he had decided for me so quickly. When I reached home I wrote a note to Mr. Haldane, intimating that he might expect to see me at the Hall to-morrow afternoon, and my letter being posted I lit my pipe, and cleaned the cages of my birds, who had grown accustomed to tobacco smoke, and gave them a treat in the shape of a bit of fresh groundsel. Buying this of a woebegone individual, with wild eyes, stubbly face, clothes in rags, and naked feet, caused me to reflect that of all the miserable wretches on the face of the earth, the men who sell groundsel are the most wretched. I asked myself the reason why, and was not discomposed because I could not find an answer. The reflection, and the question, and the attending to my birds, and the undisturbed pipe I was enjoying, convinced me that I had beaten a healthy retreat to pleasanter roads than I had been travelling since my first arrival at Chudleigh Park. The only comfort that visit had brought me was that I had made the

acquaintance of Rachel Diprose, and had
satisfied myself that she would make George
a good wife. "I'll pay for a peal of bells,"
thought I, as I went to-bed, " when the
wedding comes off."

CHAPTER XXI.

THE landlord of the "Brindled Cow" was overjoyed, or pretended to be, at seeing me.

"You're just like an old friend," said he, "and you're going to be treated like one whenever you put up at the 'Brindled Cow.' I'll defy you or any other man to find a better, or a juicier, or a better-cooked joint than you'll always find on my table. Vegetables fresh cut for dinner out of my own garden; fruit likewise; and tastier cucumbers you'll not meet with than my frame grows. To say nothing," he added, "of my wine-cellar."

I acquiesced without any display of hypocrisy, for, though but a poor judge of wine, his was certainly very good.

I enquired after Simpson, and was informed that he was in London. This rather roused

my curiosity, as Simpson had pledged himself
to spend an evening with me there on the
first opportunity. However, I did not mention this to the landlord, but said a few words
to the effect that Simpson was a bustling,
pushing man who seemed to know his way
about.

" You may say that," assented the landlord.
" If he doesn't know the ropes I should like
to see the man who does."

Having arranged to dine at the " Brindled
Cow," and sleep there that night, I proceeded
to the Hall. There I received the news that
Mr. Haldane was also in London, which
accounted for Simpson's absence from
Chudleigh. As I was making my inquiry
and listening to the answer a solemn-looking
individual presented himself, who I was afterwards informed was the house-steward. He
asked my business and name, and upon my
informing him that I had written to Mr.
Haldane and had come down on purpose to
see him, said that he was instructed to
request me, in case I arrived at the Hall

while Mr. Haldane was away, to remain in Chudleigh until Mr. Haldane returned or communicated with me. I had no objection; I wanted to get the business over as soon as possible, and not have the trouble of another journey to Chudleigh Park. Before leaving the Hall I contrived to see Rachel, whose manner was not so sparkling as usual, although she received me with affection.

"I have brought your album back," I said, "and the new one, a present from a friend. It is at the 'Brindled Cow.' Perhaps you will come and fetch it this evening; then we can have a chat."

"Yes, I will," said Rachel, "but I thought it was you who was going to make me a present of the new album?"

"A friend was with me when it arrived," I replied evasively, "and he asked me to let him buy it instead of me."

This satisfied Rachel, and she said nothing more on the subject.

"My young lady would like to see you, I

think," she said. " I will run up and ask her."

She left me and returned with the message that Miss Haldane would be pleased to see me. Upon entering the young lady's room I noticed, also, a change in her manner; there was trouble in her face, and I was sorry to see it. My present visit to the Hall had occupied only a few minutes, but there seemed to be a change in the whole air of the place. It was all life and animation on my previous visits, but now the light appeared to have died out of it. "After all," thought I, thinking of my own little home in Shepherd's Bush, "give me a cozy snuggery, with a few rooms in it, for real happiness and comfort. If I had to live in a great mansion like this I should feel like a man in a wilderness."

"I was going to write to you, Mr. Millington," said Miss Haldane, "and I am glad you have come. Can you tell me anything about Honoria?"

"No," I replied. "I have seen and heard

nothing of her. London is a vast city, Miss Haldane; one may easily lose oneself there."

"I am greatly distressed about her," said Miss Haldane. "She sent me a strange letter the day before yesterday, and I am afraid to think what will become of her, without a home or friends. Here is what she wrote. I cannot understand it."

She gave me the letter, and I was surprised at the elegance of the writing. It ran as follows :

"MY DEAR BENEFACTRESS,—

"It would add to my misery if you were to believe that I am ungrateful or unmindful of all you have done for me, and I write to beg that you will not think it is so. As long as I live I shall hold you in grateful remembrance. I have given you a base return for your kindness; had I been what you wished me to be, a good woman, I could never have repaid you. How much less can I ever hope now to do so, being what I am? You will never hear from me again. Forget me. I am not worthy to live in your remembrance. But it may happily be that I can put you on your guard against one who, I understand, is received in your father's house as a friend. He was there on your birthday, and on the day I came back to the village, and was hunted out of it. His name is Austin. Believe not a word he says. If he is already your friend, let him no longer be so. He is utterly false and black-hearted. I, who know him too well, tell you so solemnly, and I swear to God I speak the truth.

" Farewell for ever,

" HONORIA."

In silence I read the letter; in silence I returned it.

" I can hardly hope," said Miss Haldane sadly, " that you can give me any clue to this mystery, as it was only on my birthday you first came to Chudleigh. I am acquainted with no gentleman of the name of Austin, and he is not received in my father's house as a

21*

friend. Poor Honoria must be labouring under some delusion. I am so young and inexperienced, Mr. Millington, that I am at a loss for words to express myself, scarcely knowing, indeed, what it is I wish to express."

The conflicting views that presented themselves to me confused and bewildered me, man of the world as I was. One of these views was, whether it was not my duty, knowing that her friend and her father's friend, Mr. Louis Redwood, was at the same time the villain Austin who had brought Honoria to shame, to acquaint her with this fact? Honoria wished to put her benefactress on her guard; she had failed. I could do so with better effect. Should I shirk the duty? It might be that the saving or the ruin of an innocent and confiding girl's happiness was in my hands. Certain it was that at that moment I was the only person, apart from the villain himself, who was in possession of his infamous secret. Straight upon these considerations flashed the open question whether the young lady in whose presence I stood was the daughter of Adeline Ducroz, whom the hapless mother believed to be dead. For the time being I set all these matters aside; I would consider them later on. They needed steady reflection, a calm mind, a cool judgment; better to let them bide awhile.

"Mr. Millington," said Miss Haldane, "what chance is there in London for a girl in poor Honoria's position?"

"She has received a good education, thanks to you," I replied, "writes a good hand, expresses herself well, and, properly dressed, presents more than a decent appearance. There are thousands of young girls in London earning a fair livelihood in a respectable way. I don't speak of the unfortunate needlewomen who have to slave half the night through for the barest pittance, and who are the bound bondswomen of grasping sweaters."

"Grasping sweaters!" exclaimed Miss Haldane, in deep concern, as though I was introducing to her a species of unparalleled monsters. " What kind of creatures are those ? "

" Men," I said warmly ; it was a theme upon which I felt very strongly, " who grow rich by grinding their helpless creatures down and driving them to the thin line of starvation. I beg your pardon for mentioning them. A young girl like Honoria is not likely to fall into their clutches. She has too much sense——"

" I hope so," said Miss Haldane, piteously, " with all my heart I hope so ! I have always thought London a beautiful city, but as you speak of it, it is terrible, horrible ! And my poor Honoria is there alone ! Mr. Millington, I can hardly bear to think of it."

" Then don't think of it, Miss Haldane," I said. " I ought to have known better than to distress you so. If Honoria likes, she is safe from the worst side of it. Haberdashers' shops, milliners' shops, and plenty of large warehouses are filled with girls earning enough to keep them. Better still, there are the post offices, and the telegraph offices, always glad to get hold of a well-educated girl, who, once she gets a footing there, can earn good wages, and has only to respect herself to make others respect her. There are plenty of chances, Miss Haldane "

" You make me so much happier by speaking in that way! Honoria is such a girl, I am sure she is."

" Then," I pursued, warming up to my theme, and carried away by my desire to lighten Miss Haldane's heart, " a bright, presentable and clever girl, being in one of those situations, makes acquaintances who invite her home, and perhaps in one of those homes she makes arrangements to live, earning sufficient to pay for board and lodging and dress, and putting by a little in the post office savings bank. She meets a respectable young man who falls in love with her, and it happens over and over again that he is as agreeable to her as she is to him. The natural result follows. He proposes, she accepts, and they marry, and commence a new life which depends only upon themselves to turn out happily."

"Mr. Millington," said Miss Haldane sweetly, holding out her hand, " you have rendered me a great service. I am much easier in my mind about Honoria. Thank you, thank you. I am very grateful to you."

" You humbug!" thought I as, the interview ended, I was walking through the lovely park to the "Brindled Cow." " You wretched hypocrite, to buoy Miss Haldane up with hopes which you know well will never be realized! As if you had the least notion that any such happy future lies before Honoria! You could forecast what will become of her pretty accurately if you set your mind to it."

I did not set my mind to it, my thoughts running upon the past, and not upon the future. The singular resemblance between the lives of Adeline Ducroz and Honoria forced itself vividly upon me. Each had been betrayed and deserted, and their betrayers had each played his part under a false name. Notwithstanding my determination to have

no further business dealings with Mr. Haldane,
I could not but take a deep interest in the
ultimate issue of the base wrong he had perpetrated ; but it suited me much better to be
a looker-on in the game of cross purposes,
the result of which it would take a wiser head
than mine to foresee.

CHAPTER XXII.

MR. HALDANE RECEIVES A CHARACTER.

FOR the greater part of the year the village of Chudleigh was a kind of Sleepy Hollow; it was only upon rare occasions that it woke up, and exhibited symptoms of liveliness and hilarity. On my previous visits I had seen it in its latter aspect; on my present visit I saw it in its former.

It was evening. The cottage doors and windows were closed, hermetically sealed as it were; there were no gossips about; on my walk back to "The Brindled Cow" I had seen but one man, and he seemed to walk with muffled feet. There was not a soul in the bar of the public-house; the tap room, with its bagatelle table, was deserted; and the landlord, a married man with no children, and with a wife who spoke with bated breath, would have been doomed to a life of apathy

and loneliness had it not been for my com-
panionship.   He accepted with avidity my
invitation to dinner, and drank his own wine
wtth appreciation.   In the course of our
conversation, I asked him whether Chudleigh
Park was an old estate.

"Rather," he replied.   "It dates centuries
back.   You may read all about it in the
county book.   A very old family it was, gone
to the dogs many a long year ago.   Spent
their acres right and left.   Mr. Haldane's
father was a contract man : made his fortune,
bought the whole place up, stock and block,
and settled down there.   They give themselves airs they're not entitled to."

"Good," thought I ; "we are on the
road."

"There's a many here," continued the
landlord, " as look down on them as much as
they look down on us ; but they've got the
upper hand.   Old families are like old wine ;
there's a flavour about them, as a body may
say, that's wanting in new bottles.   The coat-
of-arms made in bloody wars—that's the sort

of thing all men must bow down to, whatever their politics. I can't say I'm in love with the present master. He's one man here, and another man there."

"Here in Chudleigh, do you mean, and there in London?"

"Yes, that's what I mean. He was a wild 'un in his young days, and I shouldn't like to take my oath that he's reformed. He kept his father going, I can tell you, with his wild doings and the money he spent. Right and left it went—it's in the blood of the Haldanes, I believe, to be extravagant enough on their own pleasures. It's a selfish world. There were scenes between the father and son, sometimes here, sometimes in other parts. The young rake wasn't at home more than a month or two a year; he had game to fly elsewhere."

"It's wonderful," I said, "how these things reached your ears."

"They did, somehow. Things float in the air, you know. Well, matters came to such a pass that the old gentleman swore that he

would disinherit his son.   He travelled back
to the Hall in a towering rage, and sent for a
lawyer to make a new will.   Down came the
lawyer with quills and parchment and blue
bag ; but he arrived too late.   The old
gentleman had worked himself up so that he
fell in a fit, and died, after tearing up and
burning the will he'd made in favour of his
son.   Little charred bits of it were found in
his room.   It didn't make any difference to
the son.   He was the lawful inheritor, and he
stepped in and took possession."

" A change for the better you found it," I
observed.

" Not at all ; there was nothing to be
thankful for.   For a goodish time the new
master didn't show up much at the Hall.   He
spent his money in foreign parts.   He could
do as he pleased, of course, but it didn't
speak well for him that he held himself off so.
From that day to this he's done nothing for
the village to give it a spurt.   If anything,
it's duller and slower now than when I was
a boy."

" There must have been gay doings at his wedding," I said, coming to the subject upon which I desired enlightenment.

" You're mistaken again. We knew nothing about his marriage from what took place here. We heard that he'd married in London, and we looked forward to a bit of festivity ; but he took no more notice of us than if we were cattle. It was five years afterwards that he came back here, with his little daughter. His wife was dead, we was told, and not a man among us had ever set eyes on her."

" The daughter you speak of is Miss Haldane ? "

" Yes, God bless her ! " said the landlord, with a flash of enthusiasm. " She's as much like her father as chalk's like cheese ; there's not a man or woman in the village who has an ill word for her, and who wouldn't be happy to do her a service. If she was the reigning lady things would be different from what they are."

CHAPTER XXIII.

WHO IS THE MASTER?

THE information imparted by the landlord did not assist me in coming to any definite conclusion as to whether Miss Haldane was or was not the daughter of Adeline Ducroz— always supposing, of course, that the report of the child's death shortly after her birth, was false, which was an assumption at which Mr. Barlow's client appeared to have arrived. I applied myself to the task of extracting such scraps of further information from my companion as might chance to be of use to me. Did he know into what family Mr. Haldane had married, I asked. No, he replied, he did not, and what was more, he did not care; nor did any of the villagers, he added. Mr. Haldane had chosen to ignore them, and to treat them as though they were so much dirt. What interest, therefore, was it likely they would take in a domestic occurrence, even of that importance ?

" You said awhile ago," I said, " that Mr. Haldane was one man here and another man there. You referred to his young days, I take it. He has sown his wild oats."

" Has he ? " exclaimed the landlord. " I could tell a different tale if I'd a mind to. When the parson preaches about saints and sinners it would have a better application if he pointed his finger straight at Mr. Haldane. But they don't throw stones at the rich ; it's the poor they hammer away at. What would the parson say, I wonder, if he saw the master, as I've seen him, on a racecourse, carrying on with painted ladies in a way a common man would be ashamed of ! What would he say if——"

But whatever further revelations the landlord was about to make, they were, much to my vexation, cut short by the appearance of his wife, who, opening the door unceremo niously, stood there and beckoned to him. Otherwise she neither spoke nor moved ; she simply beckoned to him. There was no resisting the mandate. Rising, after a period of imbecile hesitation, he looked at me fool ishly, and meekly followed his wife from the room, indicating to me unerringly that if ever the grey mare was the better horse within the walls of an Englishman's castle, the animal reigned here within the walls of the " Brindled Cow."

Later on I had a conversation with Rachel, which I opened by saying :

" So you and your young mistress are alone at the Hall ? "

" Yes," said Rachel, with a half sigh, " we are all alone."

" You find it dull, Rachel ? "

" Oh, no, not at all," she said promptly. " We are used to being alone. Mr. Haldane often goes to London."

" How often, my dear ? "

" Oh, over and over again. He spends more than half his time there."

" Taking Miss Haldane with him some-times, I suppose ? "

" He never does that. He goes all by himself without any warning. And he often comes back that way. I don't mind saying it to you, Mr. Millington, but if I was a young lady I shouldn't like to have such a father."

" Anything you say to me, my dear, is in confidence. I look upon you already as my daughter. And now, Rachel, the question that comes to me is, does Miss Haldane's happiness depend upon herself or upon someone else? There's a lover abroad, you told me, a young gentleman who's trying to make his fortune over the water. Does Miss Haldane's happiness depend upon him?"

" In one way it does, in another way it doesn't. You see, Mr. Millington, they can't do as they like, my young lady and her true sweetheart over the sea. There's a big stone in the way."

" The stone has a name, Rachel."

"The name's Mr. Redwood."

" Ah, Mr. Louis Redwood, the bosom friend

of Mr. Haldane. Do you mean to tell me
that he wants to marry your mistress ? "

"He has proposed to her," said Rachel.

"And she has refused him ? "

"Yes."

"How does he take her refusal ? "

"Laughs at it, won't accept it seriously,
says she cannot know her own mind, and that
he will go on loving and loving her.'

"What does her father say ? "

"He backs Mr. Redwood up. Of course
you know, Mr Millington, my young lady
doesn't tell me everything that passes between
her father and her."

"I should think, my dear, she tells you
very little ; but you've got a head on your
shoulders."

" I have to guess the best part. He talks
to her in his study, with nobody else by, and
when she comes out I see by her eyes that
she's been crying. Mr. Millington, the other
day I saw Mr. Redwood crossing the bridge
over the lake to Chudleigh Woods, and I did
wish that Mr. Redwood would tumble into the

lake, I did indeed. It's that deep and that tangled with lily roots, that it wouldn't have been easy for him to get out."

"Mr. Haldane and he being so thick together, it's likely that they often meet in London."

"From what my young lady lets fall I should say they do. What do you think I've heard whispered about, Mr. Millington—not from my young lady, but other people?"

"Tell me, Rachel."

"That Mr. Redwood is almost as much master here as Mr. Haldane himself. Mr. Redwood is enormously rich; they say he's got millions and millions. When he was quite a child, the story goes, a very, very large fortune was left to him, and he wasn't to have it till he was twenty-one years of age. All the time he was growing up the fortune kept growing up too, so that in the end it became something wonderful. I've heard that he could spend a thousand pounds a week, and not feel it. It's a pity his money didn't fall to a better man."

"It is. The whisper that's about, that he's almost as much master here as Mr. Haldane, is caused, I should say, by Mr. Haldane borrowing money of him."

"That's what I've heard. Large sums of money."

"Which indicates that Mr. Haldane is pressed for it. There are mortgages, perhaps. All this is very serious, Rachel; it doesn't make the road smoother for your mistress. Will she give way eventually? Will her father persuade her to marry Mr. Redwood?"

"Never, never, though there wasn't another man in all the wide world. She hates the very sight of him."

"Still, with her father on his side, urging her——"

"No, Mr. Millington, no. She's quiet, and gentle, and has the temper of an angel, but she can be firm as a rock. She'll be true to her lover though they may never come together; her father and Mr. Redwood may break her heart between them, but they won't persuade her to marry a man she doesn't love.

When you were with my young lady you must have noticed that she wasn't as bright as usual."

"Yes, I noticed it."

"There was a reason for it. Before her father went to London this last time he and my young lady were together in his study a good hour. A bad hour, I ought to call it, because all that day she never opened her lips to me. That didn't prevent my knowing what he'd been talking to her about; and when Mr. Redwood, who went to London with Mr. Haldane, said good-bye to my young lady, with his false voice and cold eyes, that can be as cold and cruel as voice and eyes can be, I'd have liked to poison him. That's the reason of her being unhappy. Every morning there comes from London baskets of the loveliest flowers that Mr. Redwood sends to her. They must cost a mint of money; but what's the use of 'em to a lady who doesn't care for him, and who's got more flowers growing here all around her than she knows what to do with? He only sends them to show that he's got a power over her through her father, and I hate him!"

She stamped her foot, and I could not but admire her for her loyalty, though it stood in the way of her own happiness.

"If George saw me like this," she said, presently, with a little uncomfortable laugh, "he'd think I've got a nice temper of my own. I can't help it. Right's right, and wrong's wrong."

I turned the subject by saying, "It's a pity Miss Haldane hasn't a mother living whose influence, used on her daughter's side, would be likely to turn the scale in her favour."

"It is a pity," assented Rachel.

"Does Miss Haldane ever speak of her mother?" I asked.

"Never."

"Is there a portrait of the lady in the Hall?"

"If there is," said Rachel, "I've not seen it."

"How long have you been in Miss Haldane's service?"

" Nine years."

" That was long after Mrs. Haldane's death ? "

" It must have been. I've never heard her spoken of by anybody."

It was clear that Rachel could give me no satisfactory information upon an important branch of the tangled story. Recognizing this, I began to speak of other things, and was pleased to see the vexed and anxious look fade out of her eyes before I left her for the night. Smoking my pipe I strolled along the quiet, narrow street of the village, reflecting upon the position of affairs. I had gained an insight into certain matters which had an important bearing upon the story of love and intrigue, but the longer I thought of it the more saisfied was I that I was wise in throwing up my share in it.

CHAPTER XXIV.

MR. MILLINGTON RESIGNS HIS COMMISSION.

DURING my breakfast the next morning the solemn-looking house steward of the Hall called upon me, and said that he had received a telegram from Mr. Haldane, who was on his way to Chudleigh, and would receive me at the Hall at twelve o'clock. At that hour I was received by Mr. Haldane in his study. He came straight to the point.

"I did not expect," he said, "that you would have anything to impart to me so soon, or I should not have left Chudleigh; but I was well within reach, and there has been a delay of only a few hours. I presume you have something to communicate."

"Yes, sir," I said. "I think I may safely say that I have executed the commission you entrusted to me."

"You have been quick about it," said Mr. Haldane, and I observed indications of nervousness in his manner. "Let me hear what you have to say."

"Miss Adeline Ducroz and Mr. Julius Clifford," I commenced, "were in Paris in the year you named."

"A waste of words," said Mr. Haldane, with a frown. "You were informed to that effect. Have you been employing your time in verifying the statements I made to you on behalf of Mr. Clifford?"

"Not that I am aware of, in any special way," I replied, pausing a moment to preserve my temper, which Mr. Haldane's haughtiness had aroused. "Mr. Haldane, it seems to me necessary to remind you that I did not seek this commission. You placed yourself in communication with me in the first instance, and it was with reluctance I undertook the task."

"I see no need for argument," said Mr. Haldane. "Have you any special reason for what you are pleased to remind me?"

"I have, sir. You do not speak to me with courtesy."

He stared hard at me, and paused to master his temper, as I had paused to master mine. Evidently he was not accustomed to be so addressed by those whom he considered and treated as his inferiors. He paused longer than I did, half expecting me, I think, to speak, and thus save him the awkwardness of replying in a direct manner to my independent remonstrance, but I preserved silence, and waited for him, which was another novel experience to the proud gentleman.

" I have no intention," he said, " of treating you discourteously. I shall feel obliged if you will proceed."

" I had to begin at some point," I said, " and that point was Paris. If I had not ascertained that Miss Ducroz and Mr. Clifford were in Paris at the time you mentioned, I should have come to a full stop at once. You hampered my enquiries by omitting to supply me with the name of the hotel at which they stopped."

" I informed you," he said, " that I would endeavour to obtain it, and would send it on to you."

" I received no communication from you," I said, " and I must therefore repeat that my movements were hampered. I infer that you communicated with Mr. Clifford, and that he had forgotten the name."

" You may infer as much."

" The first thing to ascertain," I proceeded, taking, I must own, a malicious pleasure in the method I was adopting, " was whether they stopped at any hotel. They did not ; they occupied a private apartment. Shall I go on from that point ? "

" Certainly from that point. Why the inquiry ? "

" Because my investigation has furnished me with particulars relating to the history of the parties before they visited Paris."

He turned pale, understanding what I intended him to understand, that I had discovered that the particulars of their previous history with which he had furnished me were false.

"We will not go into that," he said; "commence at Paris."

"When Mr. Clifford left the lady in Paris she was in a dangerous illness, brought on partly by a lamentable infatuation for drink."

"Only partly brought on by that infatuation?" he enquired, warily.

"So my information goes. She was suffering greatly from grief of mind produced by her relations with Mr. Clifford, which dishonoured her, and were more dishonourable to him."

"Are you here to preach morals, Mr. Millington?"

"I am here, sir, to relate what I have learned, in accordance with your instructions. I assume that you are anxious that nothing shall be concealed."

"Proceed, if you please."

"The malady from which Miss Ducroz was suffering led to strange developments, and it was right and proper that its cause should be traced, although such information as I have gained on that score was not the result of direct investigation. It came to me in a chance way, as it were. Her passion for drink was more a cultivated than an inherent vice, and it was produced by Mr. Clifford's treatment of her."

"A statement of that nature," said Mr. Haldane, "can be but mere hearsay."

"It might not be difficult," I retorted, "to obtain more than mere hearsay evidence upon the point. Some time after the departure of Mr. Clifford from Paris, with the precise date of which you did not furnish me, a child was born, a girl."

"Who died," said Mr. Haldane, somewhat too quickly.

"So it was reported, but the particulars of its death, such as date, place of burial, et-cetera, are wanting. Without these particu-lars the death of the child cannot be absolutely established. It is said that the baby died while the mother was in a delirious state, and she heard of it for the first time during an interval of reason when she was living in the house of a foreign doctor who undertook the cure of the disease from which Miss Ducroz was suffering."

" The poor woman," said Mr. Haldane, " ended her days there."

" She did not."

Mr. Haldane's face turned white as falling snow. " She did not ! " he echoed.

" She did not," I repeated. " With the assistance of an attendant in that house she made her escape, and finding her way to the cottage in which this attendant's sister, a married woman, resided, lived with her there some short time, until the occurrence of a calamitous circumstance which caused her to fly from the place."

" Are you certain," asked Mr. Haldane, " that you have not been pursuing a false track, that you are not confusing one woman with another ? " His voice was very strained as he put this question, and his face had not regained its colour.

" I am quite certain that I have not been

misled. There is no possible doubt as to the exactness of my information."

" Does proof of this exist ? "

I did not reply; bearing in mind Mr. Barlow's caution as to how far I was warranted to go in my disclosures, I was on my guard.

" Does proof of this exist ?" repeated Mr. Haldane. " Why do you not answer me ? "

" It is not in my power to do so," I said. " Much of my information has been gained through a third party, who has imposed secrecy upon me."

" A third party ! " exclaimed Mr. Haldane, beating the table with anger with his clenched hand. " Then you have betrayed my confidence, and have made the affair with which I entrusted you common property."

" I have done nothing of the kind, Mr. Haldane," I said firmly, " and if you do not treat me with proper respect I shall put an end to this interview immediately."

" You will put an end to this interview ? " he cried.

" I will, indeed," I said, in a calm voice.

" Had it not been for yourself I should have known nothing of the affair, and my one regret is that I ever allowed myself to be dragged into so base a piece of business. Take the blame upon your own shoulders for compelling me to address you in such a manner. You seem to forget, sir, what you owe to yourself and to others in your transactions. You seem, also, to forget that you are acting for a person with whom I am not supposed to be acquainted."

" I am corrected," said Mr. Haldane, showing the white feather, as all blusterers do when they are met with a bold front ; " but you, too, seem to forget yourself when you refer to Mr. Clifford as a person, instead of speaking of him as a gentleman."

" I decline," I said, preserving my composure, although I was inwardly somewhat chafed, " to regard him as a gentleman after what I have learned of his character ; were he present at this moment I should have no hesitation in saying so to his face. Perhaps it will be best, after all, sir, as we are both

getting rather heated, to carry out my suggestion of ending this interview.   I had no intention, when I came to see you, of doing or
saying anything except what belongs properly
to the unfortunate commission I accepted from
you.   Had you allowed me to tell my story
straight on, and to give you the result of my
inquiries without interruptions, I should not
have been provoked into the expression of
opinions."

" The interview," said Mr. Haldane, almost
deferential now in his manner, " cannot be
allowed to end here.   I will not use the word
' unprofessional,' but it certainly would not
be fair to withhold any further information
which you may have gathered in the course
of the business you undertook for me, on
behalf of Mr. Clifford.   You cannot imagine
that I have myself any personal interest in the
matter, and it is therefore ridiculous that I
should have taken up your opinions so warmly.
I apologize to you, Mr. Millington, and beg
you to proceed."

" Very well, sir.   How it was that the

rumour you mentioned of Miss Ducroz dying in the house of the doctor got about I cannot say ; I have heard nothing of such a rumour until now from your lips——"

"Say, if you please," interrupted Mr. Haldane, " from Mr. Clifford's lips."

" As you are acting for Mr. Clifford, sir," I said, with intentional emphasis, "it is one and the same." The arrow struck home, I saw, but I did not appear to notice it. "Shortly after Miss Ducroz' flight, however, from the cottage in which she had found a refuge a rumour of her death was circulated, and it was supposed she committed suicide by drowning. That rumour also, proved to be false, for some four or five years afterwards Miss Ducroz was seen alive by a woman who was acquainted with her."

" May I ask who this woman is ? "

" Mr. Clifford will remember her. She is the woman who nursed Miss Ducroz in Paris, under his direction and in his pay."

" Is it known positively that she was employed and paid by Mr. Clifford ? " asked

23*

Mr. Haldane, again, by his agitation and imprudence, laying himself open to attack.

"By whom else," I replied, "could she have been employed and paid? Miss Ducroz had no family or friends in Paris or England, and she was destitute of means. The only friend she had in the world was in America at that time—so my information goes."

"A lady or gentleman friend, may I enquire?"

If I had not been aware that he himself was Julius Clifford, his eagerness and his curiosity to learn all I knew would have betrayed him.

"A lady who had brought Miss Ducroz up as her daughter, and who took her to America. Her name is Kennedy. You will tell Mr. Clifford this?"

"I shall tell him everything you have imparted to me. It is dry work, Mr. Millington, relating so long and wearisome a story. Will you have a glass of wine?"

"No, thank you, sir," I said, as he produced wine and glasses from a compartment in the sideboard. "I consider myself on duty, and I never drink during business."

·His hand trembled as he poured out a full glass and tossed it down ; he filled another and pushed it towards me, but I did not touch it.

"You were saying, Mr. Millington——"

"That Miss Ducroz being in Paris without friends or means, and being attended by nurses and doctors, it must have been Mr. Clifford who paid the expenses of her illness."

"Is it not possible that she may have made another friend during her residence in Paris?"

"Possible enough," I replied, "but the information obtained is too precise and absolute to admit of such a conjecture. Here, sir, I come to an end of my task."

"You have ascertained nothing further with respect to Miss Ducroz?"

"Nothing further that I can speak of with certainty, or that I have the right to speak of at all."

"That is a strange answer. Can you inform me whether she is still living?"

"It is not in my power to answer that question."

"You have gained a vast amount of information in a short space of time," said Mr. Haldane, with a furtive but keen observance of me. "What methods did you adopt?"

"We never reveal professional secrets."

"There is a likelihood that you have discovered more than you have imparted to me. For instance, the name of the Parisian nurse to whom you have referred."

"Yes. Madame Pau. She met Mr. Clifford in Paris some time after Miss Ducroz's departure from that city, and it was he who informed her that Miss Ducroz and her child were dead. This is a proof that he had taken means to keep himself acquainted with Miss Ducroz's history after he deserted her in Paris"

"You are not choice in your language, Mr. Millington."

" I am speaking, sir, of Mr. Clifford, not of Mr. Haldane."

" True ; but I had no idea you were so sensitive."

" You surely did not suppose you were employing a machine ? "

" No, certainly not. I should like to ask another question or two, Mr. Millington."

" You can do so, sir, but I will not promise to answer them."

" Did your investigations lead you to any disclosures, true or false, of Mr. Clifford's acquaintance with Miss Ducroz before their visit to Paris ? "

I did not regret the opportunity he afforded me to answer and sting him. " They did. I am acquainted with the complete history of their acquaintance."

" Does it tally," he asked, " with the account I gave you of that acquaintance."

" It does not, sir. There is a very serious difference in the two versions. Remember, if you please, that I do not make this statement voluntarily. You have invited it."

"You will favour me, I dare say, with the false version presented to you by the— the——" He was in a difficulty for word to express himself—" the opposing party."

"I cannot do that, sir."

"Will money buy it from you, Mr. Millington?"

"Money will not buy it from me, sir."

"We will speak of it again by and by; my desire is to remain on friendly terms with you. What do you propose now to do?"

"I have completed my task, sir, and all I have to do is to render my account. It is here, sir, and you can examine it now, or at your leisure. You gave me a cheque for two hundred pounds. My journeys to and from Chudleigh Park, with the incidental expenses, amount to less than five pounds. I have brought the balance in cash, and shall feel obliged if you will count it."

"But, Mr. Millington," he exclaimed, in amazement, "you do not mean to say that the expenses of so wide an inquiry can have been so light? It is preposterous. Keep the money, I beg. There is your professional experience, your valuable time——"

"For which," I said, not interrupting him, and only taking his words up because he did not finish the sentence, "I make no charge. I relinquished business some time since, and should never have returned to it."

"I cannot be under any obligation to you," he said, with the mortification of a proud, vain man accustomed to have his way. "I shall insist upon paying you for your services."

"You cannot force me to accept payment," I said, with a smile; I had had the upper hand of him all through, and I meant to keep it. "It is not worth while arguing, sir. I wish you good morning."

"Stay," he cried, as I stepped towards the door, "there is something exceedingly suspicious in the attitude you have assumed. Another man would doubt whether you had behaved honestly by him."

"It is open to you to do so," I retorted.

"I certainly should not answer such an accusation."

"Or," he continued, "having accepted a commission from a gentleman who entrusted you with certain secrets, you, without warning or notice, transferred your services to some person or persons who wish to injure him."

"I will satisfy you so far," I said. "I am in the service of no person whatever, and shall not stir actively in the matter from this day forth."

So saying I wished good day again, and left him with a dark cloud upon his face, standing by the table, upon which he was beating the devil's tattoo.

"Rachel," I said, later in the day, when she was walking with me to the railway station, "I do not think you will see me in Chudleigh again. Our next meeting will be in London, and I hope it will be soon."

CHAPTER XXV.

HAVING, then, washed my hands of the affair, I bade adieu to Chudleigh with the idea that I should never visit it again unless under the impulse of curiosity. I returned to London a much lighter-hearted man than I had been for several days past; it really seemed to me as if I had got rid of a nightmare. My first visit was paid, of course, to Mr. Barlow, to whom I related all that had passed. Nothing surprises Mr. Barlow, and consequently he expressed no surprise at the information I gave him.

"It is imprudent for a man to make enemies," he said, "and it is an error into which the proud gentleman of Chudleigh Park falls rather heavily. I told you that you would have a hard task with him. He curbed himself in, evidently, being frightened by the knowledge you have gained of his character ; but take my word for it, if ever he can do you a bad turn he will not hesitate.".

"He is not likely to have the opportunity," I said, " our lines lay far apart now."

"It is those lines that lie so far apart," observed Mr. Barlow sagely, "that so often cross when least expected. High and low are closer together than you suspect. Life's a chessboard ; move a pawn wrong, and your king's in danger. That's a singular letter you tell me of from the girl Honoria to Miss Haldane. What if she should come into the play ? "

"Hardly possible," I remarked.

"In the highest degree possible," said Mr. Barlow, in correction. "Miss Haldane's future is involved in that of Mr. Louis Redwood. There are strong links between Honoria and Mr. Redwood. Mr. Redwood is in close connection with Mr. Haldane See ? "

"I am not going to worry my head," I said gaily. "I leave it to you, Barlow."

"And what they call fate," said Mr. Barlow, thoughtfully.

"I am content," I said. "I am free."

"Not quite," said Mr. Barlow. "You will hear something yet, not of your seeking, of that fellow Simpson."

Mr. Barlow was right. I think it was within a week that, standing at my street door, smoking a pipe, I saw Mr. Simpson coming down the street towards me.

"Here I am, Millington," he said, with gratified effusion, "as large as life. How are you, old friend?"

I replied that I was very well, which was true, and that I was glad to see him, which was false.

"I knew you would ¡be," he said, "after our pleasant meetings in Chudleigh. You've been down there again. Had a jolly time, I hope?"

"Pretty well," I said.

"Now, Millington, Millington," he said, in

sportive rebuke, "I wouldn't have believed it of you. 'What I like about Millington,' I said to a friend yesterday, when I was speaking of you and telling my friend what a thorough clipper you were, 'is that there's nothing double-faced about him. And that's a good deal more than you can say of most Londoners.' A jolly time at Chudleigh! No, no, my friend. Chudleigh's the beastliest hole that a man can vegetate in. Between ourselves, what took you down there?"

"Private business," I said to clench the matter."

"Ah, private business. Good to invest money there, you told me. Made up your mind?"

"Not quite."

"Likely to go down again?"

"Not at present."

"You're a close one, Millington," he said, smothering his chagrin in a laugh. "Well, I won't be hard on you. That's the advantage of being a Londoner, and living in

London. You've feathered your nest. Seen anything of Honoria?"

"Nothing. Have you?"

"Not set eyes on her. I went to see a play the other day—'Lost in London.' It was all about a young woman, too."

"Easy enough for a young woman to do that."

"To lose oneself here. Right you are, Millington. And to play one's game here without anybody being the wiser. But mum's the word, eh?"

From Simpson's state of restlessness, burning to babble, I judged that he had been imbibing a glass or two. I did not encourage him, however; I had done with his master, and had no disposition to be drawn into the net again.

"I'll tell you what," Millington," said Simpson. "I've got a night off, and I'll spend it with you."

This was cheerful, and inwardly I did not receive it gracefully; but in a sort of way I had brought the infliction upon myself by the address card I had given Simpson in Chudleigh, and without being downright boorish I could not very well shake him off.

"I will," he said. "We'll make a night of it. You shall give me a cup of tea, and then we'll go to a music hall or a theatre. I don't ask you to stand treat. We'll pay equal shares. That's only fair. When I'm in London I feel like a sailor just come ashore. No meanness about me, Millington. Here's my money,"—he rattled some coins in his pocket—"and I spend it free. What's life without jollity? I'll wait till I'm sixty before I become a chapel man."

As luck would have it, my little maid came to the door, and said that tea was ready.

"That's what I call friendly," said Simpson, clapping me on the shoulder. "After you, Millington, after you."

So I stepped back into the passage, and Simpson followed me. George, who had come home early from his workshop, ran downstairs from his room, where he was

fashioning some article for his future domestic
life, with Rachel, and pulled himself up when
he saw me in the company of a stranger.

"My son, George," I said, introducing
them. "This is Mr. Simpson, from Chudleigh
Park."

"Glad to make your acquaintance, young
Mr. Millington," said Simpson. "You're a
chip of the old block. Hallo!"

What caused this exclamation was a photo-
graph of Rachel Diprose, for which George
had made a pretty frame. It hung over the
mantelshelf. He looked at the picture,
looked at George, and George looked at
him.

"If my eyes don't deceive me," said
Simpson, "that's a fair friend of mine.
There can't be two of 'em. Pretty Rachel,
from the Hall."

"Miss Diprose," said George, stiffly.

"Yes, pretty Rachel Diprose. But I had
no notion she'd ever been in London."

"She never has been, I believe," I said,
and then I explained that some months ago

George had been down in Chudleigh, assisting in the alterations at the Hall.

"I remember their being made," said Simpson, with a lofty air, "though I wasn't in England at the time. Mr. Haldane and I were travelling in foreign parts."

"I didn't see you in Chudleigh," said George, still very stiff. The two men did not take to each other, but Simpson was more successful in concealing his feelings, whatever they may have been, than my lad.

"It's my opinion," he said, with an attempt at jocularity, tapping George on the breast, and giving him a wink, "that you're a gay Lothario, a regular Don Ju-an."

"Begging your pardon, Mr. Simpson," said George, with a frown, "I don't care to joke about ladies."

"Very proper," said the unabashed Simpson. "I take off my hat to them— and to you, young Mr. Millington. No disrespect, upon my honour as a gentleman. It's a pleasure thrown in, so to speak, to find

oneself suddenly in the presence of the picture
of a young person——"

"Of a young lady," corrected George.

"Of a young lady who lives in the same
house as I do. Show me a prettier face,
young Mr. Millington, and I'll be bound to
dispute it with you." Then he hummed an
air, and sang a line of a song commencing
with " Woman, dear woman."

Perceiving George's displeasure I put a
stop to the awkward episode by saying,
" Come along. Tea is waiting for us."

" And I am waiting for it," said Simpson,
seating himself with assumed geniality.

He did full justice to the meal, conversing
chiefly with me, for George scarcely opened
his lips. He was nettled, and he took no
trouble to disguise it.

" We're going to a music hall," said
Simpson, addressing him when he had had his
fill. " Will you join us?"

" No, thank you," said George, and I did
not attempt to persuade him.

Before we left the house I had a word

24*

with my lad, and he confided to me his opinion that Simpson was an insufferable cad, in which I heartily agreed with him.

"We shan't see anything more of him after to-night," I said. "He was rather useful to me in Chudleigh, and I've got to put up with him for an hour or two."

George threw his arm around my shoulder, and said, "All right, dad. It takes all sorts to make a world. Mr. Simpson's not one of my sort, that's all."

"Nor one of mine, my boy," I said, and with an affectionate hand-shake I went out with Simpson.

"That's not a bad little pitch of yours, Millington," said he, patronisingly, hooking his arm in mine. "Could put up with it myself. It wants just one piece of furniture to make it complete."

"And what may that be?" I inquired.

"A trim little wife," replied Simpson, and I inwardly blessed my stars that George was not with us.

"I'm past that," I said. "Too old to marry."

"Oh, I don't mean you. I was thinking of your George. Lucky young dog! I say —is it a settled thing between him and pretty Rachel?"

"Can you keep a secret?" I asked.

"Yes."

"So can I."

Whereupon Simpson burst out laughing, and vowed, as he had vowed before, that he was no match for me. I found him a trying companion; at every third or fourth public-house he made a pause, and invited me to drink, and upon my steadfastly refusing, drank alone. I thought it rather cool of him to tell me after his second glass that it was my turn to stand treat, and upon my demurring he argued the point with me, contending that we had agreed to pay equal shares in the expenses of the night's pleasures. When I pointed out to him that, so far as the emptying of glasses at public-house bars was concerned, he was having those pleasures to

himself, he replied that that was not his
fault; there was the liquor, and there the
opportunity; to which he added the inquiry
whether I did not consider his society worth
something. He insisted upon our going to a
music hall, and upon remaining till the per-
formances were at an end. At a quarter to
twelve we found ourselves in the streets, I
steadying my companion, who was by this
time in a very maudlin condition. He had
extracted from me the promise that I would
see him home, wherever that might be, and it
is seldom I have had a more unpleasant task.
He shed tears, he abused everybody, he swore
that his feelings had been imposed upon,
he proclaimed war against those who had
betrayed him.

"They had better take care," he said,
"every man Jack of them, and every woman
Jack as well—no, woman's a Jill. I know a
thing or two worth money. They had better
take care!"

"Hold up," I said.

"Hold up yourself. Why, there's them as

calls themselves gentlemen, and them as calls
themselves ladies—what are they? No better
than I am. There's names I could mention,
and things I could tell about them, that
they'd give something to keep hushed up.
Who said hush up?"

"You did."

"I didn't. It was you. Millington, you're
no better than I won't say what. There's
men as calls themselves masters, and men
they call servants. Deny it if you can."

"I don't deny it."

"Very well, then. They'd better look
out."

Thought I to myself, " If Barlow were in
my place he would worm something useful
out of Simpson." But I did not try, being
heartily sick of him.

"I know a secret or two, Millington," he
said.

"I daresay."

"I won't let on, unless they drive me to it,
and they've been near it more than once.
Butter your bread Millington, and butter it

thick. What can you say against that, you sly dog?"

"Nothing."

"If I had some people's money I'd make a show in the world. What I say is, make everything equal, give every man a chance. I won't speak against young George——"

"You had better not."

"Didn't I say I wouldn't? But why should some men have every woman, and leave other men as good as themselves out in the cold? It's an unfair division. There'll be a riot some day, and then they'll know all about. Where are you shoving to?"

He had stumbled against two gentlemen who were passing us arm in arm. They turned and looked at us, and I recognized Mr. Haldane and Mr. Louis Redwood. I do not know whether they recognized me; I wheeled Simpson aside, and they did not accost us, but the chance encounter did not add to my comfort; my apparently confidential association with Simpson could easily have been interpreted into treachery.

" Did you see who those gentlemen were ? "
I asked.

".I didn't, and 1 don't care "

" They were your master and Mr. Redwood. You'll hear something of this to-
morrow."

" Shall 1? Who cares? When I've got a
night off I do what I like with it. Perhaps
he'll discharge me, perhaps he won't. I defy
him. That for my master ! "

He snapped his fingers, and I was well
pleased presently when, getting entangled in
a crowd gathered to witness a night brawl,
the opportunity was afforded me of giving
Simpson the slip. His subsequent adventures
on this night were no affair of mine. I should
have been delighted to hear that they had
ended in the lock-up.

CHAPTER XXVI

HONORIA MAKES HER REAPPEARANCE.

MR. BARLOW being anxious that I should omit none of my experiences in connection with this history, I have at his request added another chapter, which will be my last.

During the six months that elapsed after my " night out " with Simpson I saw nothing more of him. There was a sufficient reason for our not meeting. He and his master had gone abroad, and for the most part of this time remained out of England. I did not pay another visit to Chudleigh Park. Miss Haldane wrote to me once about Honoria, but I had no news to communicate, and I replied to that effect. These were the only letters that passed between us. George, of course, kept up his correspondence with Rachel Diprose, but their marriage appeared as far off as ever. It did not lessen my lad's

love for his sweetheart, nor, as her letters
proved, hers for him. From these letters I
gathered that Miss Haldane's life at Chudleigh Park was rather lonely. She received
no visits, and paid none, a sign that she had
made no friendships of an enduring nature
among those of her station. Once only did
George go to Chudleigh, to see Rachel; he
spent a Sunday there, and stopped at the
"Brindled Cow"; that he did not go again
was due to Rachel, who thought it best that
he should keep away—for her young mistress'
sake, I believe. I took the blame of this
upon myself. George was my son, and as I
was not in favour with Mr. Haldane my lad's
appearance in Chudleigh might have been
misconstrued.

"You will be an old man, and Rachel an
old woman," I said to George, "before you
come together."

"Not quite that, I hope, dad," said George.
"Things will be all right before long."

I did not have much faith in long engage-
ments, and so I hinted to George; but he

appeared to be satisfied that nothing could occur to prevent him and Rachel being true to each other.

"She is worth waiting for," he said, "and it's no use fretting."

Mr. Barlow also was at a standstill; he had made no further progress in the affair upon which he was engaged, for although he made no fresh discoveries he was still in commission. It was his opinion that Mr. Haldane had left England to escape detection. I remarked that if this were the case Mr. Haldane must have had some suspicion that an enemy was working against him. Mr. Barlow concurred, saying that something must have reached Mr. Haldane's ears which put him on his guard. My old partner paid me regular visits, which George and I returned. He and his wife had grown very fond of George, and about once a week we all took supper together, at Barlow's house or mine. On one of these nights, when we walking from his house, Barlow, who liked a little walk after supper, being with us, he asked me if I had anything particular to do to-morrow. I answered, nothing.

".I want you to spend an hour with me," he said. "Come to the office between two and three."

I presented myself accordingly and we turned from Surrey Street into the Strand, and there took a 'bus to the Marble Arch. I may mention that it was the height of the season, and London was very gay, by reason of a Royal visit, which set society circles in a flutter.

"I am going," said Mr. Barlow, "to take you to Rotten Row.

"Anything special going on there?" I asked.

"We shall see," was his reply.

This was enigmatical, but I knew that Barlow seldom did anything special without a special reason. In the 'bus he volunteered another piece of information.

"Mr. Redwood is in London," he said.

"And Mr. Haldane?" I inquired.

"I cannot say, but it is very likely."

Arriving at Rotten Row we found a good place by the rails, and watched the panorama of fashion as it passed by and repeated itself on horseback and in carriages.

"It is a favourite pastime of mine," said Mr. Barlow. "I like to see the swells doing duty."

"There are plenty of them," I said, "who don't seem to be enjoying themselves much."

"It is a sad pleasure to many," said Mr. Barlow, "especially to the carriage swells; but it is a duty they owe to society to show themselves. Look at that lot."

There were three elderly ladies in the turn-out, and unutterable weariness reigned on their faces, which were worn and pasty with late nights. I smiled, and said I would sooner be what I was.

"Bunkum," observed Mr. Barlow. "If you were a swell you would do likewise."

It did not escape me that all the time we were talking he appeared to be looking out for something not in the common way, and a sudden lighting up of his features revealed to me that it was approaching. In a handsome victoria, the appointments of which were absolutely faultless, sat a young lady, who as she came closer to us, caused the blood to rush into my face.

"Ah," said Mr. Barlow, who was observing me closely as the victoria approached.

"Barlow," I cried, seizing his arm, "you remember my telling you about the girl Honoria I brought to London from Chudleigh Park?"

"Perfectly," he replied. "I don't forget much."

"I could swear," I said, "that the very girl is sitting in that carriage."

"Wait till she comes round again," said Barlow.

I strained my eyes till I saw her in the distance. She was richly dressed, and leaned back in her carriage with the born negligent air of a lady of fashion. That one so beautiful should attract universal attention was not surprising; and indeed she was very beautiful. No trace of despair was on her face, which bore the expression of one accustomed to admiration. Hats were raised to her, and now and again a mounted cavalier carolled by her side, and exchanged salutations. Some she received graciously, some coldly, but even in her graciousness there was an air of disdain and power to which all appeared to submit. No lady saluted or acknowledged her, but I noticed that most of them looked furtively, even admiringly at her. As she passed us the second time she happened to turn her eyes in my direction. They rested on my face, but there was no sign of recognition, although she gazed at me steadily.

"Well?" questioned Barlow.

"It is Honoria," I said.

"It is the name she is known by," said Barlow. "That is why I asked you to accompany me to-day."

I sighed, thinking of Miss Haldane. "And this is what she has come to," I said.

"Yes," said Barlow. "She has the world

at her feet, this girl whom you saved from drowning in the lake of lilies."

We lingered by the rails till she came round a third time, and again her eyes travelled in my direction, and rested a moment upon me, as before. My presence did not appear to discompose her; she was as completely self-possessed and composed as if we had never met.

"Come and have a cut of mutton with me," said Barlow, an hour or so later, "at the namesake of a friend of yours in the Strand."

We strolled to Simpson's, and had a good old-fashioned English dinner there, and afterwards went to a theatre where they were playing a rattling farce, mis-called comedy. Strangely enough—it is always so; it never rains but it pours—in the principal box sat Honoria, dressed with elegant taste, with flashing diamonds upon her. We were in the pit, and had a good view of her box, in which, between the acts, appeared a succession of gentlemen swells. I saw but little of the farce, my attention being centred upon this girl, once so low, now so shamefully high.

"Let us get another peep at her," said Barlow, when the curtain finally fell.

We hurried to the lobby entrance of the stalls where the visitors were waiting for their carriages, and where I witnessed a comedy, as unexpected as Honoria's appearance in Rotten Row earlier in the day. As she came out to her carriage, leaning on the arm of a gilded youth, Barlow nudged me smartly, and there, to my surprise, was Mr. Louis Redwood, gazing at the girl he had betrayed. He hesitated only a moment, and then, with a confident air, with outstretched hand, and with a smile upon his face, advanced towards her. She gazed at him with superb disdain, and without bestowing any further attention upon him, turned her back upon him. In another moment she was in her carriage, and the smile on Mr. Redwood's face vanished. The "cut direct" had been perfect, and people were laughing at him.

Barlow and I talked of the incident as we walked away, and I expressed my surprise at Mr. Redwood's eagerness to be friendly with Honoria.

"Know the world better, old friend," said Barlow. "The girl is a marvel of beauty, and men of loose fashion are running wild after her."

"Yes," I said, "it is her beauty that made him so eager."

"Wrong once more," said Barlow. "It is not her beauty that attracts him now. We run after the unattainable; we despise what is easily obtained; we value things more or less, not for what they are, but for the ease or the difficulty in getting hold of them. If the girl were as ugly as sin it would be the same to Mr. Redwood. She is a rare commodity, and he sighs for possession. You are familiar with a little fish called the sprat?"

"Of course I am."

"A most delicate, most appetizing fish, but being plentiful can be bought for a penny a

25*

pound. Make them as scarce as red mullet, and the world would rave after them. As it will one day after Honoria, if she plays her cards well."

I make no comment on this scrap of philosophy. My task is ended, and I lay down my pen.

The Third Link—Fashioned of Letters Written by Lovers and Friends, False and True.

———

CHAPTER XXVII.

LETTERS.

From Frederick Palmer, Dunedin, Otago, New Zealand, to G. Palmer, Esq., Westminster Palace road, London.

My DEAR FATHER,—

My last, and first, letter written to you from Australia was necessarily short, because I had just one hour to make up my mind whether I would accompany a friend I made on the passage out, who, hearing of the discovery of gold in New Zealand,* urged

---

* It may be necessary to state that Frederick is not chronologically correct in his reference to the discovery of gold in New Zealand, but this is a license of which a writer of fiction may legitimately avail himself.

—THE AUTHOR.

upon me that it was just the place in which fame and fortune could be quickly won. I allowed myself to be persuaded. Here was a new land, with new opportunities and glowing possibilities waiting for me. " Done with you," I said, and an hour later we were on board the *Eureka*—what a name! it was an augury of success — with four or five hundred other adventurers, bent on the same errand as myself. Only I had a special motive which others lacked to spur me on, the love of the sweetest girl that ever drew breath since Eve roamed with Adam through the groves of Paradise. I see you, dear old fellow, shaking your head, and sighing, " Dreams, Fred, dreams! Will you never awake?" And I answer, " No, never." Why? Because I am not dreaming, because I hold fast to Hope, the fairy that touches reality with golden light, that shows me the road to the future, when you, and I, and one whom I devotedly love, will be living together the happy life. Father mine, what made you a painter and a poet? The solid, serious view of a man's life and ambition, or that very fairy Hope which, with the higher spirit Ambition, directed you into paths which made you what you are? You lost your fortune. Well, I am going to make another for you and her. The diary I kept on the passage from England to Australia, and which I sent you with my first brief letter will show whether I lost courage on the way; and let me say now that I am stouter-hearted than ever, and that though my pockets are poorly lined, I am confident that what you call dreams will at no distant day be proved to be realities. I am coming back to you when my fortune is made. I am coming back to her I love; years of delight and happiness are before us; arm in arm, and heart in heart, we shall talk of the harvest the wanderer has reaped for those near and dear to him, and you shall say, " Well done, Fred; you were right and I was wrong— happily so."

Now, arriving in Dunedin safe and sound, the question was what should I do? The pilot who boarded us and conveyed us into Port Chalmers had set the whole ship in a state of excitement by reports of wonderful discoveries of new goldfields. Transferred at Port Chalmers into a small steam tug that took us through the loveliest bay in the world to Dunedin jetty, the news was confirmed. As for scenery I cannot describe it ; my sketch book is filled with themes for future work— and glory—to say nothing of the gold pieces which will roll in to sweeten success. A picturesque tumbledown wooden jetty, to be replaced one day by a stately stone structure (for I see the grand future already looming), crowds of people burning with the gold fever, wooden shanties hastily thrown up to transact business in, the old Scotch settlers scarcely knowing whether to approve or not of the invasion of heterogeneous human particles, but at the same time, with proverbial wisdom, turning the honest penny and making hay while the sun shines, adventurers bronzed with travel discussing the chances in the unformed street, the continual animated

going to and fro, the loading of drays, the
clattering of horses, the perspective glimpses
of civilization's soldiers marching over the
distant hills — imagine all this, and paint
pictures from it. But a man's eyes must
behold these scenes to properly depict
them. They are like a page of old time
history, full of romance and colour. Said
the friend in whose company I journeyed
hither, " Off we go to morrow morning to the
goldfields ; in six months we come back with
our fortunes made." But pride and prudence
stepped in and whispered in my ear. Said
prudence, " How can you start on such a
journey with empty pockets ?" Said pride,
" Don't humiliate yourself by a confession of
poverty." Therefore spake I to my friend,
" I cannot accompany you ; here in this
primitive city of wonders will I stay awhile,
and rest my weary feet, and refresh my spirit,
and strengthen my body for future toil."
(What have you to say, father, to the style
biblical ? Does it sit well on me ?) My friend
remonstrated, argued, pressed, but I was

firm, and away he went, the nomad, in company with a hundred or two others, straight in the eye of the sun. I to a newspaper office and there enlisted for a pound a day. So behold me, a budding journalist, bent on work and shekels. Here I have been three weeks, and am sixty shillings the richer, after paying board and lodging—no joke, though mutton is two-pence a pound. Humph! Rather a lugubrious outlook. But this is only a beginning. When you build you must commence with single bricks. Two water-colors are near completion, and the next question will be to find purchasers. Are there art worshippers here, rich patrons eager to draw large cheques as an evidence of the wedding of grinding commerce and intellectual refinement and taste? The landlord of the principal hotel, who boasts of taking a thousand pounds a day across his bars, suggests a raffle. By the Beard of Venus which never grew, am I descended so low? But why should I fume? Are there not art lotteries in England, and what is a lottery but a raffle? It is a distinction without a difference. We must not be over nice in these new lands. The mail for dear home does not go out for twelve days, and before it closes I shall be able to tell you the result of my first art-labor in this world-end Arcadia. I break off my letter here, and go to bed, to dream of you and my dear Agnes.

Now to finish my letter, dear old fellow, the mail closing to-morrow morning. The raffle has come off. There was more than a spice of grim humour in it. The pictures were hung in the public room of the hotel, flanked by a couple of hideous German chromos. Said I to myself, said I, "My paintings will teach those honest barbarians, will educate them, will prepare them for future works of glory." Puffed up with unbecoming pride, I lingered in the public room of the hotel, to take a lesson from the critical opinions of entranced admirers. The pictures were scarcely glanced at. "We'll wake them up," said my friend and landlord, and beneath the great achievements was placed a placard with a written intimation that the first original local paintings by an eminent artist would be raffled on Saturday night at half-a-crown a chance. I remonstrated with the landlord, who had put up the placard without consulting me. "What do you object to," he asked. "To the low terms of subscription," I replied, employing the most dignified phrase that occurred to me. "Quite enough," said the landlord. "Look at those pictures"—pointing to the hideous German chromos—"can you compare them with yours?" "No," said I honestly, "I cannot." "More can I," said the landlord, "and they only cost me four pound a pair." Well, the raffle came off. Contemplate the figures. Forty subscribers at half a crown a head come to exactly five pounds. The frames for the pictures cost me fifty shillings ; "treating" the subscribers on the eventful night, three pounds six shillings ; total debt, five pounds sixteen shillings ; total loss, sixteen shillings ; and my meritorious paintings. "But you've made a start," said the landlord, congratulat-

ing me on the venture. Truly I have. Farewell art awhile. I must come down to earth,
for this rate of progress resembles the man
walking on ice who for every step forward
slides two backward

Now, my dear father, I want you to let me
know all about my dear Agnes—how she is,
what she says, how she looks, et cetera, et
cetera, et cetera. What does she think of
my diary of the passage across the seas!
Heavens! What a waste of water divides
us! But I look forward, I look forward,
and am not in the least discouraged. As
you know, I have bound myself to write to
her only once in every six months, and the
first term is not yet expired. There is nothing
to prevent you sending her my letters to you,
and she will know from them that my love is
unchanged, that it can never change, and that
the one dear hope of my life is to call her
wife. Tell her that I am going to be practical.
Fortunes are being made on the goldfields. I
shall go there, and make one for her. Then
I can ask her father for his consent to our

union, which I cannot do, with any chance of success, while I remain poor. I have the fullest faith in her, as she has in me. God bless her, and you, my dear father. Address your letters to the post office in this city,

Your affectionate son,

FREDERICK.

From G. Palmer, Westminster Palace road, London, to Frederick Palmer, Esq., Post Office, Dunedin, Otago, New Zealand.

MY DEAR BOY,

Your two letters, one from Australia, the other from New Zealand, with the diary you kept on the passage out, have been safely delivered, and I reply to them by the first opportunity. I sent them to Miss Haldane, Chudleigh Park, under cover to Miss Rachel Diprose, in accordance with your directions, and I have received them back, with a note from Agnes, in which she sends you as many kind messages as the fondest lover could desire. She says she is well, and she writes as you do, cheerfully and hopefully, but I

have no means of discovering how she looks.
Mr. Haldane and I are cousins, it is true, but
as wide as the waste of waters between you
and home is the gulf between him and me.
To go to Chudleigh Park without an invitation would be courting an affront, and would
not advance your cause. You know how
fully and completely I sympathize with you
in your hopes of the future, and I shall say
nothing to cast a shadow on them. Your
account of the two pictures you painted is
amusing, and you are wise in your resolution
to throw aside the brush, and to engage in
those pursuits in which money is most easily
made. With my own example before me, I
should have given you a commercial education, which would have made you fitter for
your present career. However, like you, I
hope for the best. I am painting two pictures
for the Academy; is not that a proof that I
have still with me Hope, your fairy, and that
I do not intend to beat a retreat from the
ranks in which many better men than I are
struggling? Cherish that fairy, my dear boy

—always open your arms and your heart to it ; whatever the result, it will brighten your days and nerve your arm. How well I remember my first Academy picture! It is a good many years ago, and I can count on my fingers the number of my pictures that have gained admission since that time. I have told you the story often—how it was sold, how I used to walk the streets with a light heart, thinking that *I* had painted the picture of which some influential papers spoke highly, and that a few of the persons who passed me might possibly know that I was the artist. I never sold another picture off the Academy walls, but I am waiting, my boy, I am waiting, and you or I will make a fortune yet. Am I not writing to you with an airy spirit? Ah! but my dear lad, you little know how I miss you.——But there, I am not going to say a word to sadden you; better burn the letter than send it to my wanderer across the seas. Until you went away I used to grumble at time passing so quickly, but now it cannot pass too quickly for me, for it will hasten the day of our reunion. Everybody who knows you inquires after you and sends you the kindest messages. God bless and speed you!

Your loving father,

G. PALMER.

From Frederick Palmer, Otago, New Zealand, to Miss Haldane, under cover to Miss Rachel Diprose, Manor Hall, Chudleigh Park.

MY DARLING AGNES,

At last the first six months are over, and I can write to you. I wonder sometimes how it was that I gave you the promise to write only once in every six months, and then my wonder vanishes when I think it was because you asked me, fearing that if I wrote frequently it might set your father against me before the day arrived when I shall feel myself warranted to ask his consent to our union. My dear Agnes, I think of you day and night, and it is your dear image that cheers my lonely hours and sustains my courage. You have heard from my father of my unpromising start, which had something comical in it, and of my determination to seek fortune on the goldfields. Here am I, then, in my digger garb, with beard well grown, and so unlike my London self, that were you to meet me in the street you would hardly recognize me.

Now, what shall I say to you, my darling girl—I, upon whom fickle fortune has not yet smiled? I am in a Tom Tiddler's ground, and every day I hear of men drawing grand prizes. It will be my turn one day; it must be my turn, for I have you and love on my side, and the charm will be sure to succeed. The truth, then, is, my darling, that I am no richer at this moment than when I first set foot on these shores. I am in good health, and I do not intend to lose heart. Up early in the morning, working till sunset, whispering your dear name as a charm, and going to sleep with your image in my mind. I have a comrade, and we manage to find enough gold to keep us, but there is the chance every hour of finding a big nugget or striking a " rich patch." It is only a matter of time: the longer good fortune is a-coming, the brighter is her smile when she shows her face. And I woo her, and woo her, and whisper to the invisible goddess, " For my dear girl's sake, come, now, for the sake of the dearest, dearest girl in the world!" I give you my word that I utter these words in my most coaxing accents, and that I go to work again refreshed and strengthened by them, with the conviction that my pleadings will not be in vain. We live in a tent like the patriarchs of old, a fitting simile, for at no very great distance from us is a sheep and cattle station where I am always welcome—I walk there sometimes of a Sunday, a matter of twelve miles, easily done on the soft bush roads in three hours—the owner of which, an Oxford man like myself, is master of seventy thousand sheep. As I gaze upon his enormous flocks I think of biblical days when Jacob wooed Rebecca, but I do not want to wait so long for my dear girl. Words are poor to express all I feel; dearly as I loved you when I left England, I love you still more dearly now. You are my good genius, my good angel, ever by my side.

26*

I walk with you through the woods, I sit on a fallen tree and talk to you, your spirit is in my heart. Think of me always as your true and faithful lover, who never lays his head upon his pillow without thanking God for the priceless blessing of your love. My dear girl, does your father know? Have you told him yet? Keep nothing from me. He cannot object to me on the score of birth; it is only that dreadful bugbear, money, money, money. I will work and wait for it, and you shall hear from me that our wishes are realized. Do not doubt it, darling. I do not. With undying affection, believe me, ever your faithful lover,

FREDERICK.

From Agnes Haldane, Chudleigh Park, to Frederick Palmer, New Zealand.

MY DEARLY BELOVED,

Your letter made me happy, so happy! I have read it so many times that I must know it by heart, but I keep on reading it, for it brings you nearer to me. Be sure,

my dear, whether you are absent for a long
or a short time, I will be true to you,
and will wait for you—yes, till I am an old,
old woman. I ought to tell you, dear, but
you must not distress yourself about it, for
nothing can change me. There is a gentleman who has been here a great deal, and
papa would be glad if I encouraged his attentions. His name is Mr. Louis Redwood, and
I do not like him, though papa wishes me to.
I only tell you of him because I think it right
you should know all that takes place. And
now you must know something else. I have
been considering a certain thing lately, and
when papa comes home (he has been abroad
some time) I shall tell him all about you and
me. I feel that I am acting wrongly in keeping our secret from him; it is my fault, I
know, that this was not done at first, but I
was a little afraid of the way papa would take
it. Seeing now what it is right to do, I shall
have the courage to do it, and I am sure you
will approve. Well, now, this is all about
myself, and nothing about you. What a

wonderful life you are living, and how strange
it must all seem to you! I get all the books
I can about Australia and New Zealand, and
I know a great deal now about those
countries. Rachel Diprose, my maid—such
a good girl!—has an uncle there, and she
says it is a splendid life, though she is all for
London, where she has never been, but where
her sweetheart lives. He is ready and anxious
to marry her, but the good, foolish girl will
not hear of it. She will not leave me, she
says (unless I turn her away and I shall never
do that), until I am married. It is not of the
slightest use to argue with her; she has made
up her mind and has passed her word, and
she says she will die rather than break it. If
I needed a lesson in firmness, which I don't,
dear, she would teach it to me. I hardly
know whether this letter will satisfy you; but
perhaps you will be satisfied when I say that
I am yours, and yours only, and that you
may be sure I shall never love you less than
now. My mind is easier now that I have
determined to tell papa everything when I see

him. Good-bye for a little while, dear
Frederick. I pray for you always, I think of
you always.

> With constant love,
>> I am ever yours,
>>> AGNES.

*To Mr. G Palmer, Westminster Palace road,
from Mr. Haldane, Manor Hall, Chudleigh
Park.*

SIR,—

Information has reached me that
your son, Mr. Frederick Palmer, has taken
advantage of my absence during my daughter's
visits to London to pay his addresses to her
without my knowledge or sanction. Such
conduct is scandalous and unbecoming a
gentleman, and hearing of it now for the first
time I write to you without an hour's delay
to put a stop to the proceeding. I understand
that your son is in one of the Australian
colonies, and that he has had the presumption
to open up a correspondence with my
daughter. If I were acquainted with his

precise address I should write to him direct,
to the same effect as I am writing to you, and
I demand his address from you in order that
I may express to him my opinion of his conduct. You, as a father, will not contest my
right to views in which my daughter's welfare
is concerned, and to the carrying of them out
in the way I deem most suitable. Expecting
to receive from you your son's address in the
colonies, and your concurrence that the clan-
destine intimacy shall instantly cease,

I am, your obedient servant,

C. HALDANE.

*To C. Haldane Esq., Manor Hall, Chudleigh
Park, from Mr. G. Palmer, Westminster
Palace road.*

SIR,—

I am in receipt of your letter, the
contents of which I will communicate to my
son. From the relationship between us, and
my standing in society, though far from a
rich man, I might reasonably have expected
that you would have expressed yourself in

different terms, and I shall certainly not afford
you the opportunity of addressing my son in
like manner. Therefore I refuse to give you
his precise address. But as many weeks must
elapse before he can hear what you have
written to me upon a matter as important and
dear to him as it is to you, I lose no time in
correcting your opinion of his character.
My son is a gentleman, upright, honourable,
and delicate-minded, and that you should
pronounce his conduct "scandalous" reflects
no credit upon you. That he loves your
daughter as a gentleman, and hopes to win
her, is true, and the only bar I can perceive
to the happy result of an honourable attach-
ment is the difference in our circumstances.
If, notwithstanding your letter, it should be
his happy fate to be united to your daughter,
I, who know my son as no other man
knows him, and who knows something of
the sweet and amiable qualities of your
child, have no hesitation in declaring that
their happiness would be assured. It is best
that I shall say no more. Time, which

tries all, is a beneficent healer, and I place
my hope in it.

Faithfully yours,
G. PALMER.

*To Mr. G. Palmer, Westminster Palace road,
from Mr. Haldane, Manor Hall, Chudleigh
Park.*

SIR,—

Your reply to my letter is imperti-
nently worded, and is intended as an insult.
I shall know how to guard myself and
daughter from its implied defiance to my
wishes. You refuse to give me your son's
address; I will obtain it from my daughter.
You are a dealer in sentiment and cant, and
your son doubtless takes after you.

Your obedient servant,
C. HALDANE.

To C. Haldane, Esq., Manor Hall, Chudleigh Park, from Mr. G. Palmer, Westminster Palace road.

SIR,—

Letters addressed to my son at the Post Office, Dunedin, Otago, New Zealand, will reach him in that colony.

Faithfully yours,

G. PALMER.

CHAPTER XXVIII

From G. Palmer, London, to Frederick Palmer, New Zealand.

MY DEAR BOY,—

The necessity of giving you pain is forced upon me. Enclosed you will find copies of four letters, two addressed to me by Mr. Haldane, and my replies thereto. I do not know if they will come upon you as a surprise; you will certainly be unprepared, as I was, for Mr. Haldane's communications, and you must act the manly part, and meet them with a man's courage. The form in which he expresses his sentiments is not a graceful one, but we will set that aside; it shows that he is bitterly, strongly in earnest, and it proves him to be a hard, unfeeling gentleman. Here before us, my dear boy, is a battle of heads and hearts, and it has sometimes happened that hearts have won. You

will perceive from this remark that I do not
advise you to lay down your arms : it is a
serious matter for a daughter to go against
her father's wishes, but after all it rests with
you and Agnes.   If she sides with her father,
you have no alternative but to retire ; if she
says, " I will be true to you," then it will be
for us to decide how to act in this grave
crisis in two young lives.   Remember that
you have always your father's love ; through
weal and woe I am faithful to my dear
boy.

Ever your loving father,
G. Palmer.

*From C. Haldane, Manor Hall, Chudleigh
Park, to Frederick Palmer, Dunedin, Otago,
New Zealand.*

Sir,—

I have with some difficulty obtained
your address from your father, and I now
write to you to express my opinion of your
conduct in clandestinely following my
daughter with your attentions, and in carry-

ing on a correspondence with her without
my sanction. No man of honour, no gentleman, would pursue such a course, and I shall
have no difficulty in exposing your true
character to my child. In her name and
my own I demand that you instantly cease
writing to her or communicating with her in
any way whatever. Should you presume to
disregard my wishes I shall know how to deal
with you.

Your obedient servant,
C. HALDANE.

*From Agnes Haldane, Chudleigh Park, to
Frederick Palmer, New Zealand.*

MY DEAREST FREDERICK,—

I write to you in great grief. Papa
came home last week, and I told him all.
My dear Frederick, there was a dreadful
scene ; he spoke of you in a way that I could
not listen to quietly, and I defended you ;
but what could I say when he asked me if I
considered it proper for a daughter to enter
into such a serious engagement without the

knowledge or consent of her father? He said I could make some amends for my fault by promising him that I would not marry without his consent. Even if I had not felt that I had acted wrongly I should have given him the promise; and I was encouraged, too, because his passion seemed to be over. "It is a binding promise, remember," papa said, and I answered that I would keep to it. But O, dear Frederick, what have I done? Papa says that he will never consent to our marriage, and now I am very unhappy, not only for myself but for you. I seem not to have a friend except my maid, Rachel, and she cannot do anything to help me. But can any one do that so long as papa is against us? I can only hope that he will be kinder when he finds out that I cannot obey him. Dear Frederick, I seem to be doing wrong whichever way I act. Papa stands on one side of me and you on the other, and I am pulled both ways at once. I will be true to you, indeed, indeed I will, but if I had some one to counsel me I should feel happier.

God bless you, dear Frederick. With all my love, believe me to be always yours,

AGNES.

From Frederick Palmer, New Zealand, to C. Haldane, Esq., Manor Hall, Chudleigh Park. .

DEAR SIR,—

I am in receipt of your letter, and I deeply regret the risk I run in adding to your displeasure when I say I cannot comply with your desire. It was wrong, I admit, in the first instance, to enter into an engagement with your dear daughter without your knowledge, but my sense of self-respect revolts against the opinion you express of my behaviour. I do not seek to excuse myself; whatever blame attaches to this unhappy affair is mine alone; but what I did was not deliberately done; my feelings hurried me on until words were spoken which cannot be recalled. May I appeal, dear sir, to your recollections of yourself when you were young, when a man's judgment is the slave of his heart, and feelings are involuntarily born within him which he cannot resist? There is no difference in our rank, and I beg you to excuse me when I say that money cannot confer distinction. I love your daughter truly and devotedly, and it would be the aim of my life to make her life happy. I have come to this distant land in the hope of bettering my fortune, so that I might be able to offer her a home befitting her station. Up to this day I have not been successful, but fortunes are being made all around me, and I have not lost the hope that brought me here. You ask me to give up your daughter, and with all respect to you my answer must be that I cannot do so unless she bids me. Sustained by the belief that her heart is mine I shall live on the hope that time may soften your feelings towards us, and that the happiness to which we look forward may yet be ours.

I am, dear sir, faithfully yours,
FREDERICK PALMER.

From Frederick Palmer to Miss Haldane, under cover to Miss Rachel Diprose, Manor Hall, Chudleigh Park.

MY DARLING AGNES,

What shall I say to you — how shall I write? If it were not for the last lines in your dear letter I should despair, but while we are true to each other there must be light in the future which we may hope will shine upon us when our trials are happily ended. Your father wrote to me in anger, and I have replied to him, temperately I trust. My darling, I say to you what I said to him—I cannot give you up unless you bid me. To spare you a sorrow I would sacrifice my life, and gladly would I take all this suffering upon myself if it were in my power. You say you seem not to have a friend except your good maid Rachel. Do you forget my father? He is the noblest, the truest of men, and there is nothing you could call upon him to do that he would shrink from doing. Heaven forbid that I should counsel you against your father, that I should ask you to forget a daughter's duty. Your have promised him not to marry me without his consent, and he should be content with this promise, knowing that we must both abide by it. The misery of my position is that I am no farther advanced than when I first landed in this colony. If I could go to him with fortune in my hands he would surely relent; it is money only that separates us. Heaven will listen to our prayers, for they spring from faithful hearts. If I could only be near you—if I could only see your dear face! But I must not. I will not repine. I sometimes think, "If my dear girl were poor there would be no difficulty; she would be equally dear to me." So that you see there are circumstances in which poverty would prove a blessing. But it is useless speculating in this fashion : what we have to contend with is not what might be, but what is, and I must be hard and practical, for your sake and mine. My darling, to the last hour of my life I will be

27*

true and faithful to you. I shall ever be what I was from the first moment I saw you.

Your faithful lover,

FREDERICK.

From Louis Redmond, Esq., Queen Victoria Mansions, Westminster, London, to C. Haldane, Esq., Brevoort's, New York, U. S. A.

MY DEAR HALDANE,

What the devil has sent you off to America so suddenly, and why did you not ask me to accompany you? Here I am just arrived from Nice, after a cursed bad time at the tables (dropped eighteen thousand in three days; very refreshing!), with a little imp in petticoats to make it worse, to find the Haldane bird flown without having the grace to offer the shelter of its wings to its best friend. But perhaps the said wing is sheltering something more attractive than a man of the masculine gender. What is it, Haldane? Another little affair? At your age too! I am ashamed of you. Didn't relish leaving

my bullion behind me at Monte Carlo, and
the aforesaid petticoated imp has been playing
high jinks with yours truly. I'm tired of
her tantrums and have made up my mind to
settle down. This is leading up to what
follows; opening the case. as the lawyers
say.

Talking of lawyers, there it is, you see?
I'm a devilish clever fellow to introduce the
firm so deftly. Lamb and Freshwater,
Bedford Row. We know those chaps well;
they've made a fortune out of me and mine,
but I must do them the justice to say that I
never got into a difficulty they didn't get me
out of. But that's not the point, which is,
mortgage. Chudleigh's a pretty place, but I
don't want to foreclose. I'd sooner it fell to
me in an amicable way, and for five weeks
out of the fifty-two it would do, with the
right sort of spirits about one. Not a bit of
good without a pretty hostess to do the
honours. You're of a shrewd breed, and can
guess what's coming. Fact is, I'm tired of
waiting as the song says.

Lamb & Freshwater, the dear (the very dear) solicitors, pointing to the mortgage deeds, murmur, " One hundred and twenty thousand!" which you will admit is a good round sum, and insinuatingly ask me, " What is to be done?" That's the rub, Haldane. Am I in want of the money? Do my last pair of boots require soleing and heeling? I think not. My thieving valet has not called my attention to the state of my wardrobe, so I infer I am still presentable. My bank book's all right, and the manager receives me with smiles. I am so beastly rich, you see. Then why do I lug in the trifling sum you owe me? Not the only account between us —excuse my mentioning it, but my back's up. I'm not going to be trifled with much longer. It wouldn't take the twentieth part of the time to tell you all this (and more to come) that it does in writing it down fairly and squarely, but if you will run away when you're wanted I'm bound to grind it out on paper. There's that other sum you want paid in to your bankers before the end of the half-year. I'm the most complaisant fellow in the world; I can spare it, and you shall have it, but you must give me, besides the moderate interest, another sort of *quid pro quo.* I want a sweety, Haldane, and I want it all the more because it's been promised me so long, and as matters stand it is just as far off to-day as it was at the beginning. (See Prayer Book.) I am sick of playing patience. There's a ripe peach on your wall, and I'm growing dangerously savage. Plain writing's the order of the day. Therefore, boon companion and friend of my soul, take timely heed.

I cannot recollect that we have ever come to a perfectly formal understanding as to this very lovely and luscious peach. In friendly conversation I have pointed to it and spoken about it, and your pleasant answer has been " Gather it, my dear Louis; I give it to you freely; consider it yours." Consider it mine! I have wooed it, coaxed it, tempted it, paid incense to it, prostrated myself before it, and there it hangs upon your wall for any hands to pluck when it is in the humour to say, " I am willing ; " but to me those words have never been spoken. My dear Haldane, you must put pressure upon your peach, you must exercise authority, or—take the consequences. In plain set terms I ask for your daughter's hand. It is yours to command, hers to obey, mine to worship and endow. Do not doubt that I am prepared to be very liberal in the settlements. A longer delay will be dangerous. Act instantly and firmly, and your difficulties are over. We will kneel at your feet, and you shall give us your blessing. We shall make a pretty couple, and you will gain in me another child whose virtues you have already appreciated. My wife shall work you a pair of slippers, or buy them ready made, and in your old age you shall have a corner by our fireside. Could any man be more filial ?

I must request you to reply to this letter without delay. Lamb & Freshwater are getting impatient, and a simple fellow like myself must submit to be guided by his legal advisers. If you take my advice you will come home very soon ; your presence may be required. Meanwhile I subscribe myself, prospectively,

Your dutiful son-in-law,

LOUIS REDWOOD.

Cable message, from Haldane, New York, to Redwood, London.

I write to my daughter by this mail, ordering her to receive your addresses. Letter to you, also, by this mail. Shall be home in four or five weeks.

From C. Haldane, Esq., New York, to Louis Redwood, Esq., London.

MY DEAR LOUIS,

Were I inclined I might object to the tone of your letter, but my feelings for you are entirely friendly, and you should be satisfied by this time that you have my cordial consent to your proposal. Agnes is very young, and girls of her age are inclined to be coy, therefore you must not be too impatient. I will leave it to your discretion

to speak or write to her upon the receipt of
this letter (I am writing to her by the same
mail), or to wait till I return to England.
You are generally inclined to follow your own
bent, and I have no doubt you will do so in
this instance; therefore, I do not advise you.
As to the money matters between us I rely
upon the assurances you have given me that I
shall not be pressed or harassed.   I have
had bad luck for a long time past, and for my
son-in-law that is to be to play the Shylock
would be infernally unfilial.   Lamb & Freshwater be hanged; you are the captain of the
ship.   Restrain your impatience, my dear
Louis; Rome was not built in a day, and
your experience of women must have taught
you that they are often difficult to manage.
Pay that money in to my bank as soon as
possible; rolling in coin as you are, there
can be no possible question of inconvenience.
You lucky rake!   What would I not give to
be in your shoes?

Yours truly,
C. HALDANE.

From C. Haldane, Esq., New York, to Miss Haldane, Manor Hall, Chudleigh Park.

MY DEAR DAUGHTER,—

I am about to write to you on a very serious matter, and you must understand that I expect a dutiful compliance with my wishes. After all I have done for you I have the right to command, but I would prefer that you should give a willing consent to my wishes.

Mr. Louis Redwood, a gentleman and a man of honour, has formally proposed for your hand, and I have consented to your union with him. In the last conversation you and I had on this subject I disputed your right to oppose me in a matter upon which I am so much better a judge than yourself. You are young, and inexperienced; you know nothing whatever of the world and of the traps which designing men set for a lady of your birth and position. You must be guided by me; Mr. Redwood is of a suitable age; he moves in the best society; he is good-looking and enormously rich.

My estates will be settled on you; you will
have a house in London, with surroundings
which cannot fail to make you happy; and
your affianced will gratify every wish of your
heart.   There is not a lady in England who
would not joyfully accept the offer which Mr.
Redwood makes to you.   He does us great
honour, and you are most fortunate to have
won the love of such a man.   I have, I think,
said enough to induce you, if you need
inducement, to listen to him favourably, and
to make me happy.   Fully convinced that
you will offer no further obstacles to an
alliance upon which I have set my heart, I
am, my dear Agnes,

Your affectionate Father,

C. HALDANE.

*From Louis Redwood, Esq., Queen Elizabeth
Mansions, Westminster, to Miss Haldane,
Manor Hall, Chudleigh Park.*

MY DEAREST AGNES,

I have your father's sanction to
address you on a subject very dear to me, and

I hope to you. I flatter myself that you can have mistaken my attentions as little as you can doubt my devotion. As a writer of love-letters I do not think 1 should shine ; as a husband I should. I lay my heart at your feet ; open Paradise to me, by consenting to become my wife. This is not so bad for a commencement.

You shall have everything you wish ; I will refuse you nothing ; an establishment in town, in the country, on the continent. If you want to stop at home, we will stop at home : if you want to travel, we will travel ; you shall command me in every way. I dare say you know I am rich, for which I thank my stars : spend my money for me, and make me a happy man. I might have waited till your father returned home before making my proposal, but I could not stand the delay. I am burning to know my fate ; do not keep me in suspense. Kindly accept the accompanying trifles. I have selected them with the greatest care, but if the stones and settings are not to your liking we will have

them altered. I am urging your father to
hasten home ; I want him to advise me about
carriages and horses. You will have to come
to town when he returns, and your taste shall
be followed in everything.

Your devoted lover,

LOUIS REDWOOD.

From Miss Haldane to her Father.

MY DEAR FATHER,

I am very, very sorry that I cannot do
as you wish. I do not love Mr. Redwood,
and I cannot marry him. Were my heart not
engaged I could not accept him ; in my own
defence I am forced to say that I do not
believe him to be a good or a sincere man. I
may be wrong, but I cannot help saying what
I feel. My dear father, his riches would not
make me happy ; I would not mind being
poor with the man I love ; with Mr. Redwood,
my life would be a life of deceit and misery.
I beg you to forgive me ; the thought of your
displeasure makes me very wretched ; I will
do anything you ask, but this I cannot. I

have already promised you that I will not marry without your consent, and if you withhold it I must remain as I am. My dear father, I write in love and duty, but I cannot be false to the dictates of my heart.

Your loving and unhappy daughter,

AGNES.

From Miss Haldane to Louis Redwood, Esq.

DEAR SIR,

I feel honoured by the proposal you have made to me, and regret that I cannot accept it. I have told my father so in a letter. Trusting you will meet another girl who will be worthier of you than myself, I remain,

Yours respectfully,

AGNES HALDANE.

From Louis Redwood, Esq., London, to C. Haldane, Esq., New York.

DEAR HALDANE,—

I enclose your daughter's reply to my proposal, and I hope you will like it. If I'm not mistaken you will find it an expensive piece of paper. Short and sweet, is it not—

damned short and sweet? But I'll make it short and sweet for you if she doesn't take it back—and pretty quick, too! I sent her a model of a love-letter; took me almost a day to put it in form; I worried over it like a terrier; and this is the answer she treats me with. She doesn't even condescend to mention the case of jewels I sent her—cost me over a thousand pounds—but despatches them back to me without a word, the case unopened. I know it hasn't been opened, by a little trap-mark I set on it. I'm not much of a Christian, Haldane, any more than you are yourself. When I get a slap on one side of my face I show my teeth, and those who abuse me live to repent it. What do you think? Lamb & Freshwater have been on to me again about that mortgage; and you'll receive a notice from them by this mail. Funny coincidence, is it not? I have not paid that money you ask for into your bank —that's funny, too. Fact is, I'm riled.

Do I give up the hunt? No—and here's your chance, your only chance, if all you've told me is true. Perhaps you'll talk of my throwing you over. I don't throw you over, but you know what the inducement has been. And now the prize is to be snatched from me. Very well. I'll have some satisfaction for it; I'll sell you and your daughter up. See how she likes that. I'm not blind or deaf, Haldane; there's another fellow in the way. If you aren't clever enough to shunt him off, take the consequences. It's quite as much your affair as mine. I'm playing the magnanimous in not retiring from the field at once, and leaving the affair entirely in the hands of Lamb & Freshwater, but I confess I don't like to be beat, and I'll hold on a while longer. Lamb and Freshwater inform me that the mortgage must be paid off or renewed this very day two months. If you can't cash up you know my terms for renewal, so be wise in time and bring your precious daughter to her senses. If you are not a fool you will take the first steamer home, and I wish you joy of your reflections during the voyage.

Yours most unamiably,

LOUIS REDWOOD.

Cable message from Haldane, New York, to Redwood, London.

Shall be in London in a fortnight. Meanwhile have written to my daughter. It will be all right. Lamb & Freshwater's notice mere formality, I suppose.

From C. Haldane, Esq., New York, to Miss Haldane, Manor Hall, Chudleigh Park.

AGNES,—

You have distressed me terribly. Mr. Redwood's offer must be accepted—*must,* I say. There is no alternative. You compel me to disclose what I hoped to keep always from you. I have been a good father to you, and wished to spare your feelings, but I must now tell you the plain truth.

For years past I have been in difficulties, and only one person has stepped forward to save me. That person is Mr. Louis Redwood. He has advanced me large sums of money, which have been spent in maintaining my position, and yours. When he first assisted me

you were a child, and there could have been
no thought of love-making in his mind, but as
you grew up he learnt to love you. The
kindness he showed towards me was perfectly
disinterested, and had you not been in exist-
ence he would have continued to be my
friend. But you have angered him, and the
child I nourished is now my enemy. My fate
is in your hands; if you do not accept Mr.
Redwood I shall be a ruined man. You must
perform your duty. What you say about
your heart being engaged is childish and
absurd; what you say about Mr. Redwood is
ridiculous and unjust. He will make you a
good husband; he will give you a position
that titled ladies will envy. You have no
choice in the matter; the attitude you have
assumed is unwarrantable. Understand that
I will allow no further hesitation or evasion.
I command you to write to him instantly,
retracting that refusal. He is willing even
now to prove himself our best, our only
friend. If you fail in your duty I discard
you. My home is no longer yours if you are

rebellious; you must seek one elsewhere. Upon receipt of this letter you will send me a message by cable to allay my anxiety. I enclose a form, so that you will have no excuse for neglect. Two words will suffice: "I consent.—Agnes." Then you will have done your duty to me and to yourself, and you will live to bless the choice you have made.

Your father,

C. HALDANE.

Cable Message from Miss Haldane, Chudleigh Park, to C. Haldane, Esq., New York.

I cannot, I will not consent. I have heard something of him which fills me with horror.

AGNES.

From Rachel Diprose, Manor Hall, Chudleigh Park, to George Millington, Shepherd's Bush, London.

MY DEAR GEORGE,—

Whatever is going to become of us I have not the least idea. Everything is at sixes and sevens, and a good deal worse than that. My dear young lady is in a dreadful way, and goes about like a ghost. Her father is here, and so is that hateful wretch Mr. Redwood, and I wish they were both at the bottom of the Red Sea. I want to know why some people are allowed to live. I am sure it is wrong, and if I had my way I would make it right. Yes, I would. Now what do you think of me? You had better give me up, George, dear.

Ever since my young lady got that letter without any name to it, telling her such dreadful things of Mr. Redwood and that girl Honoria, she has not been like herself. What a monster he is—and is Honoria any better? There! I haven't patience with things! Before that my dear mistress was worried enough. Her sweetheart over the seas, there was something the matter with him, and she sighed and cried till she made me cry and sigh too; and now her father has come home, and Mr. Redwood with him, and between them they are fretting my young lady's life out of her. When they are having dinner I wish bones would stick in their throats and choke them, the wretches, that I do!

To make things worse, her sweetheart across the seas can't do anything to help her. He went away to make his fortune, and it is as far off as ever. George, dear, what is to be done? I can't think of anything; can you?

What a foolish, foolish question! What can you or anyone do while those two fiends —yes, George, fiends—go on as they are doing? They're the masters, and between them they'll break my dear young lady's heart unless—— Well, don't be surprised at anything that occurs. We never know what we can do till we are put to it. Not that it will bring you and me any nearer together. I'm speaking in riddles, you'll think. I can't help it—I can't help anything.

They are trying to buy me over. Mr. Haldane comes to me first, and says that my young lady does not appear to be very well, and has got some nonsensical notion in her head about a young man far away, and what

a stupid thing it is, and what a lovely time
there is before her with Mr. Redwood for a
lover and a husband, and how beautiful it
will be for me when I'm living in London with
my lady, and going to the theatres, and
having all sorts of pleasures, and how there's
a gold watch and chain, and two beautiful
silk dresses waiting for me on the day she is
married at a grand church in London, with
heaps of bridesmaids, and orange blossoms,
and white veils, and all that, and all that, till
there's a regular buzzing in my ears. But I
press my fingers to them, and the humming
goes away, and I curtsey and say I hope my
young lady will be happy, and then he goes
away, thinking he's made it all right with me.
But if Mr. Haldane thinks he has bought me
over, and that I am going to do anything to
make my young lady marry that detestable
Mr. Redwood, he's reckoning without his host.
No; not for fifty gold watches and five
hundred silk dresses would I do it. Then
Mr. Redwood sneaks up and says, "Rachel,
you're a sensible girl, and I'll bet a

hundred to one you've got a sweetheart, and
a lucky chap he is "—(I've my own opinion
about that George)—" and he'll be a luckier
on the day I'm married to your mistress, for
there's five ten pound notes waiting for you
when the wedding comes off." It's all waiting
for me, gold watches, silk dresses, and
ten pound notes. Enough to turn a poor
girl's head, but it doesn't turn mine. I'm
not to be bought by Mr. Haldane and Mr.
Redwood. If we ever marry, George, dear,
you're going to have a very foolish wife, but
as it's not at all certain that we ever shall
marry you needn't worry over it beforehand.
Shall I scratch out the last words? No,
because I have never deceived you before,
and I won't deceive you now. My dear
young lady will never, never marry Mr. Louis
Redwood, and she has made a promise that
she will not marry anyone without her father's
consent. It isn't at all likely that he will give
his consent to her marrying her sweetheart
across the seas, even if he was to come home
rich, and as my young lady therefore will

never marry at all, neither will I. There it is, in a nutshell. We shall both die old maids. I am so sorry for you, dear old George ; but never you mind ; there's as good fish in the sea as ever came out of it, and there's hundreds and hundreds of young ladies ready to jump at you the moment you hold up your little finger. Good-bye, dear. Give my love to your dear father. As things are, I musn't send you any.

Your true and loving sweetheart,

RACHEL DIPROSE.

From George Millington, London, to Rachel Diprose, Chudleigh Park.

MY DEAREST RACHEL,—

Your letter is rather confused, but I understand it very well, and I can see clearly how matters stand. You are rather a whirl-wind, but I am not, and when we are married your temper and mine will make a very good mixture. My dear, I am really sorry for the unhappy state of affairs at the Hall, and if I could do anything to help sweet Miss Haldane

I'd fly to do it. I wish you would tell her so. Not that it will be of any real use, but when anyone is in trouble it does them no harm to know that there are people who feel for them. About your dying an old maid, Rachel—no, Rachel, I set my face against it; I can be as determined as you, and determined I am to marry you, if not this year, next, if not next year, the year after. So don't let us have any more talk about other young ladies ready to jump at me. They may jump; I shan't hold out my arms to catch them.

I will tell you what father has found out through his old partner, Mr. Barlow. Mr. Redwood has got Mr. Haldane under his thumb, and can sell him up at any minute he pleases. That's the secret of their friendship, and of their both trying to force Miss Haldane into the match. Father wants me to say this. We have a home, not very grand, certainly, but very comfortable, and there it is for you and your young lady, if ever you should be driven to London for a time. Of course it is a wild idea, but father says, " Just you put that down, George," and I have put it down.

I am at work on the most beautiful dressing table you ever saw, all of inlaid wood, with your name, Rachel, inlaid on the top. I am getting quite a houseful of furniture ready for us. Father sends his love to you, and his respects and sympathy to Miss Haldane. As for me, I can't find enough love to send you, but all I have is yours. Send me another letter very soon.

Your faithful sweetheart,

GEORGE.

From Rachel Diprose, Chudleigh Park, to George Millington, London.

MY DEAR OLD GEORGE,—

You are a dear good fellow, that you are. After I posted my last letter to you, I said to myself, " Whatever will George think of me for writing such a hotch-potch ? " for so it seemed to me when I sent it off. But I was worked up into a regular pitch of excitement, and there's no one I can speak my mind freely

to but you. It is such a relief. I know you
are patienter than I am, and better tempered,
and nicer altogether, but if things should ever
happen to come right I'll try to make it up to
you, I will, indeed, George, dear. The idea
of your calling me a whirlwind! but I am
one, I feel like one. If I could whisk my
young lady up now, and carry her over the
sea to her sweetheart there, and see the
wedding-ring on her finger, it would be done
without waiting to consider about it. That's
the way a foolish woman talks, isn't it,
George? If she could do this, if she could
do that—as if wishing was the least bit of
good in the world?

George, dear, things are worse than when I
sent my last letter. Mr. Redwood goes about
as smiling as ever, making presents almost
every day to Miss Haldane, presents that she
never looks at unless she's forced to; but Mr.
Haldane is looking very black. Yesterday
morning I was going through the passage
when I heard Mr. Haldane say to my young
lady, " You have made up your mind to ruin

me." " No, papa," my young lady answered ;
" only I will never, never——" That is all I
heard : I didn't dare to wait because the door
was open, and they were talking close to it.
Last night it was settled that there was going
to be a grand ball here, and that any number
of ladies and gentlemen are to be invited. My
young lady looks very white over it. How is
it all going to end? What a good, patient
boy you are to make all those beautiful things
that will never be used, for a house that will
never be furnished! The sight of my dear
young lady's unhappiness drives me into
saying things I should never dream of. I will
write to you again about the ball. I told Miss
Haldane what your father said about your
house, and she asked me to thank you, and
said I ought to be a happy girl ; and I should
be, George, dear, if she was. Good-bye, dear.
With love to you and your father,

Your true sweetheart,

RACHEL..

From George Millington, London, to Rachel Diprose, Chudleigh Park.

My dearest Rachel,—

Just received your letter, and write a line before going to work. Don't be so low spirited; everything will come right. I can see that things are coming to a crisis with Miss Haldane, and that something of the greatest importance will soon take place. I do sincerely pity her, and I admire you for your loyalty to her. You are staunch to her; you will be staunch to me. What better proof could I have? Only, my dear girl, if you cannot prevent things you must not let them break your heart. That would be foolish—and not fair to me, because your heart belongs to me. I beg to inform you that it is my property, and you must take care of it. The dressing table is finished, and I am planning a washstand to match. I must be off; can't afford to lose more than half an hour. With love that will never change and never grow less,

Your true sweetheart,

George.

From Rachel Diprose, Chudleigh Park, to George Millington, London.

MY DEAR OLD GEORGE,—

You are foolish to be so obstinate, but I must not blame you for it. No other girl would. But, George, what *is* the use of your going on making things that will never come in use? Isn't it a waste of wood? And to work my name in them, too! That is more foolish still, unless you can meet someone else named Rachel that you would like to propose to; then there would be some excuse for you.

The ball came off last night, and nobody who was there will be likely to forget it. You said that something of the greatest importance would soon take place. George, it has.

There was a grand dinner at half-past eight o'clock. At half-past seven my young lady was not dressed. She was sitting in her room in her morning dress, and I was waiting by; one of the dressmakers was there as well.

" You will be late, Miss Haldane," the dressmaker said. My young lady did not speak,
and the dressmaker went away, and came
back presently with Mr. Haldane. " How is
this, Agnes?" he asked, and his face was
white with passion. " Papa," she said—but
he stopped her, and sent us from the room.
In about five minutes he came out—we were
standing in the passage—and said to me.
" Go in, and dress your mistress." We both
went in, and without Miss Haldane or me
saying one word the dressing was commenced. About twenty minutes past eight
Mr. Haldane knocked at the door, and asked
if she was ready. " In five minutes, sir,"
said the dressmaker. He came again then,
and sending the dressmaker away—he is a
proud gentleman, and hates a scene—he
called Mr. Redwood in. In came that
scorpion, with the most magnificent bouquet
that ever was seen. He smiled and bowed,
and offered the bouquet to my mistress ; she
did not look at him. " Take the flowers,
Agnes," said Mr. Haldane. If a steel tongue

could speak the voice would be like his. My
young lady turned to him for just one
moment, and took the bouquet. Then the
scorpion offered her his arm. "Agnes!"
cried Mr. Haldane, and she put her fingers on
the scorpion's arm. Then they left the room,
and I tidied it up, and the dressmaker came
back with the ball dress and arranged it. I
went down to the kitchen, and all the
servants were talking about Miss Haldane,
and saying she looked like a corpse. I held
my tongue, and let them talk. I heard that
my young lady and Mr. Redwood were
engaged, and that the engagement would be
announced that night by Mr. Haldane at the
ball or the supper. Dinner was over at half-
past ten, and my young lady came back to
dress for the ball. I didn't see what I am
going to tell you; it is only what I heard
afterwards, but I am sure it is all true, and
exactly as I describe. Miss Haldane danced
only one dance, and that by compulsion.
The scorpion was her partner. If others
had pity for her, he had none. He did not

leave her side, and did not dance with any other lady. At about three o'clock in the morning, when the supper room was full of people, Mr. and Miss Haldane and Mr. Redwood being there next to each other, Mr. Redwood said something quietly to Mr. Haldane, and was heard to say, "It is my wish." Then Mr. Haldane got up to make a speech, and everybody was quiet. He asked them to fill their glasses, and when this was done he said, "This ball is given in celebration of an event which I have the happiness to announce to you. It is the engagement of my daughter and Mr. Louis Redwood, and I ask you to drink to their health and happiness." Well, just as they were about to drink my young lady rose, and held out her arms, and they waited to hear what she had to say. She spoke in a very low tone, but they say that every word was distinct. "My father is mistaken," she said; "Mr. Redwood and I are not engaged." They put down their glasses, and looked at each other, not knowing what to make of it.

Mr. Redwood never lost countenance. He smiled and said they must have observed that Miss Haldane was not well; the fatigue of the night had been too much for her; and he asked them to excuse her. Then he offered her his arm to take her to the ball room, and she turned her back upon him, and accepted the arm of another gentleman, but she had not gone two steps before she sank to the ground fainting. She was carried to her room, where I was waiting for her, and in a few minutes she recovered her senses. I put her to bed, and as she begged me to do so, I lay down by her side, and we were soon asleep. She went to sleep first; I think she was happier because she had made up her mind to something. After breakfast a servant came with a message from her father that he must see her at once in his study. "Tell my father I will speak to him here," she said, and when the servant was gone she told me to go to the inner room, not considering perhaps that I could hear every word that passed between them. I did

29*

as I was told, and presently her father came to her. "Now," he said, and his voice grated on my ear like the scraping of a knife, "be good enough to explain the meaning of your conduct last night." "I think, papa," she answered, "that you should give me an explanation of yours. Why did you tell the people that I was engaged to Mr. Redwood?" "It is the truth," he said, and she said quite boldly, "It is not the truth, papa." "How dare you say that to me," he cried, very furious, "when you know it is my wish?" "I dare, papa," she said, "because nothing on earth can ever force me to marry Mr. Redwood. If you knew what I know about him you would not wish me to marry him. You would abhor him as I do." "I know everything about him," Mr. Haldane said. "You have some silly, romantic notions in your head, and it is time you got rid of them. There must be an end to this nonsense. You do not know what is best for you; I do; and I say you will be a happy woman when you are Mrs. Redwood." "That," said my young lady, "I will never be. I will rather beg my bread in the streets." "It may come to that," said Mr. Haldane. Well, they went on talking, Mr. Haldane fuming and begging, and she keeping firm. At last he said, "Tell me plainly what your objection is to Mr. Redwood?" "I have more than one objection," she said. "Even if I loved him, which I do not, and never shall, he has acted towards a poor girl in a manner so base and dishonourable that I would never again take his hand in friendship." "I asked you to speak plainly," her father said. "Read this," she said, and I heard the rustling of paper, and knew she was giving him the unsigned letter she had received about Mr. Redwood and that Honoria. Everything was quiet while he read it; then he said, "This is the work of a scoundrel who has a grudge against an honourable gentleman. He shall answer for himself." He went away, and came back soon with Mr. Redwood himself. "Mr. Redwood," said Mr. Haldane to my young lady, "will tell you that the letter is a tissue of falsehoods. "Quite false, I assure you," said Mr. Redwood, in his smooth voice: "and now we will forget what is past. Why did you not tell me of this letter before? It would have explained what I have never been able to understand—why you refused me." My young lady answered very steadily, but in a lower tone. "My father puts me to shame by bringing you here, and speaking of the letter. I cannot discuss it with you. I have told you repeatedly, Mr. Redwood, that your attentions are distasteful to me. I beg you not to persecute me any longer." "All's fair in love and war," said Mr. Redwood. "That I have proposed to you heaven knows how many times is the strongest proof I can give of my love and devotion. Honour me by accepting my hand and fortune." "For the last time, Mr. Redwood," said my young lady, "I decline your proposal." "You can't deny," said Mr. Redwood, after a little pause, he was speaking now to Mr. Haldane, "that I have made a good fight of it. I give you twenty-four hours. If you can bring your daughter to reason within that time I stand to my offer. If not, I leave the matter in the hands of Lamb and Freshwater." Then he went away, and her father said, " If you do not consent to accept Mr. Redwood before this time to-morrow I turn you from my house. You will find another home; this will be no longer open to you." " I will never marry Mr. Redwood, papa," said the poor young lady. " You have one day to decide," said Mr. Haldane. " I have decided, papa," said my young lady very sweetly. " Forgive me." But he turned away savagely from her, and slammed the door behind him.

I told my young lady that I had heard everything, and she said she had not thought of it when she asked me to go to the inner room. " But I need not trouble to tell you now, Rachel," she said. " You heard what my father said, and I have made up my mind what to do." Then and there she told me that she was going to leave her father's house the very next morning—that is to-morrow,

George—and intended to go to London, and try to live there. " But how, my dear mistress," I asked, " how will you get a living in that big place ? " " Oh," she answered, " I can paint, I can draw, I can sew, I can teach. Perhaps by and bye my father will forgive me." Upon this I told my young lady that if she went to London I would go with her, and work for her, whether she would allow me or not. The idea of her working for herself ! She doesn't know what is before her ; I do, although I've never been in London. She wouldn't consent to it at first, she wouldn't as much as listen to it, but I said it would not be right or proper for her to live in London all by herself, and that she must have some one to look after her, and who could do that better than I could ? And at last, George, she consented ; and she kissed me, and said such beautiful things to me, and we had a good cry together, and so it is all settled.

I am going to run out and post this letter, and I shall write you another letter from Chudleigh, perhaps late to-night, and another when we get to London. I send you my love, and your father, too, though I don't see what is the good of it.

Your affectionate Sweetheart,

RACHEL.

From Rachel Diprose, Chudleigh Park, to George Millington, London.

MY DEAR OLD GEORGE,—

It is all over; we are going to leave Chudleigh Park, to leave the old house; and whether we ever see it again who can tell? I shouldn't wonder if the sky was to fall on the top of the earth; I shouldn't wonder at anything.

Her father came to her this morning when I was with her, and said, without ordering me from the room as he always does when he sees me there, " Have you considered what I said to you yesterday ? " " I have, papa," said my dear mistress. " What is your answer ? " he asked. Then it was my mistress who sent me away, and I went and walked up and down, wondering how it would end, and whether he would have the heart to turn her out of the house. After a little while I saw Mr. Haldane and Mr. Redwood walking in the grounds together, and knowing my dear mistress was alone I went up to her. She was whiter than ever, and she said, " I am going away, Rachel," she said, and then I knew that it was all over. " To-day, Miss ? " I asked. " Yes, to-day, Rachel," she said. " To London ? " I asked. " Yes, Rachel," she said, " to London." " When shall we start, Miss ? " I said. Then she began to talk to me again, and said that I had no right to sacrifice myself because she was in trouble—just think of her speaking of sacrifice to me, George, dear!—and that it was my duty to look after myself. I said I was looking after myself, and that I had thought the matter well over, and didn't intend to leave her service. Well, George, dear, the long and the short of it is that she had to give way, and when she confessed that my company would be a comfort to her, my heart was light as light could be. Then I

helped her to look over her things. She's
got any number of dresses, but she wouldn't
take them with her; she chose three plain
frocks, and some other bits of dress she can't
do without, and I packed them in a trunk,
and smuggled in one or two things when she
wasn't looking. " There's your jewellery,
Miss," I said. Would you believe it, George,
she wouldn't take a single thing her father
had given her ? " But they're yours, Miss," I
said, " your very own, to do what you like
with." " They belong to my father now," she
said, " I have no right to them. I'm not
penniless either, Rachel ; I've got over twelve
pounds in my purse, and that will keep us
ever so long if we are careful." I asked her
if there was any friend in London that she
would go and ask advice of, and she said
there was, and mentioned Mr. Palmer's name.
Mr. Palmer is her sweetheart's father, George,
and I was glad to hear that she had thought
of him. He is not well off, but that doesn't
matter ; she will have another friend to stand
by her as well as me. When my own box

was packed I went to the steward and got what wages were due to me. Mr. Redwood was there, and after I had signed for my money he asked me if I wanted a place. " When I do," I said, " I sha'n't come to you for one." He only laughed, and said that some of us had a lesson to learn, and perhaps they'd be sorry when it was too late. I don't think that man has a heart.

The train doesn't start for nigh upon two hours, so we have plenty of time. What do you think my poor mistress is doing? Taking leave of her home ; going to her favourite rooms and places in and out of the house, and saying good-bye to them. I wanted to go with her, but she said she preferred going alone, so I came up here to write my letter to you. A few minutes ago I looked out of the window, and there was my young lady walking slowly along, looking at the trees and the flowers, with all her heart in her eyes. Not far from her stood her father and the scorpion. She turned towards them, but they never moved. The scorpion took out his cigar case, offered it to Mr. Haldane, and then lit his cigar, with a look in his eyes that made my blood boil. Seeing they would not take any notice of her, my young lady moved slowly away, while they went on talking and smoking. What a pair! I hope a judgment will fall on them some day, and that I shall be there to see it. That's all the harm I wish them.

There was our boxes to take to the railway station. We couldn't carry them, and it was quite as likely as not that orders had been given that nobody was to assist us. So, not to be outdone, I went down to the " Brindled Cow" and told the landlord to send up a carriage for us.

Now, George, don't you go blaming me because I don't call upon you to meet us at the railway station in London. I know what I'm doing, and I'm doing everything for the best. And don't you go and think hard things of me for not asking you to help us; if you do I'll never speak to you again as long as I live. Besides, I've got no claim on

you now; it's all over between us, for I can't
expect you to go on waiting for me for ever;
so, George, dear, consider yourself free, and
look out for another girl.   You won't have
any trouble in finding one.   You will always
be my friend, won't you ?   Good-bye, dear.
With a thousand thousand kisses, and with
my eyes brimming over, thinking of you and
everything, I remain,

     Your loving and unhappy
        RACHEL.

*From Rachel Diprose, 5 Warrington Street,
E.C., to George Millington, Shepherd's
Bush.*

MY DEAR OLD GEORGE,—

  Here we are, in London, and now I
can write to you.   We are settled down in
four rooms, two on the first floor, and two on
the second.   The front room on the first floor
is what we call the living room; the back
room we use as a kitchen; the two rooms on
the second floor are our bedrooms.   So we
are quite comfortable, at least I am.   But

oh, what a change it is for my dear young lady! Not that she complains. There she sits while I am writing to you, with some work in her hand she is trying to do, and not making a very good job of it. " I must learn, Rachel," she says, and I don't try to dissuade her, for it's good for her to have something to do, whether she does it right or not ; it prevents her from thinking too much. Now I must tell you about our going away from Chudleigh Park.

There was the carriage from the " Brindled Cow " at the door, and there was the landlord himself to drive it, and the ostler to help down with our boxes. It isn't often the landlord of the " Brindled Cow " drives a customer in any of his traps, and I knew he'd done it this time in honour of my dear young lady, and I was grateful to him for doing so much.

George, dear, all the servants were outside in the grounds, and they all came up to her and said, " Good-bye, miss, and we hope we shall soon see you back again." It was a trial to her, but she bore it bravely. "Good bye," she said, and she shook hands with them all, and took the flowers they had gathered for her; and the carriage, too, was full of flowers. I could have kissed every one of them, I could, though they were not all females; I did kiss them that were, for they said good-bye to me as well, and what little differences we'd had at one time and another were all forgotten and forgiven. There was a great St. Bernard dog, my dear young lady's favourite of all the dogs in the place, the dog that was hers and nobody else's, that I knew she'd have given the world to take with her, but didn't dare, for fear of her father. She knelt down and put her arms round his neck and kissed him again and again; and George, dear, in all the people that were standing about there wasn't a dry eye. Yes, there was; I am telling a story. The scorpion was there, standing on the steps of the Hall, as if he and nobody else was master there—and perhaps he is. He was smoking, of course; he is always smoking, and I wish he'd smoke himself into a fit that he'd never recover from. He was looking on, cool and smiling, and seemed to enjoy it all. Oh!—but there, I'd better keep myself in! If there's such a thing as justice in heaven or earth, it will fall on him one day and break his wicked heart. He stood there as cool as you please, and when we were in the carriage he was brute enough to raise his hat to my dear young lady. Chud—that's the name of the dear great dog—was quite close to the carriage, and I thought if I was in my mistress's place I'd tell him to jump upon the scorpion and tear his heart out. And Chud would have done it, too.

Then the carriage began to move off, and the servants ran after it to the gates of the Park, and there was the lodge-keeper and his wife with more flowers, and every man there had his hat off, and every female servant had her apron to her eyes. The rector came out with his wife and children, and they shook hands with my mistress, and asked her to

write to them, and whether she promised or
not I can't say, but she kissed the children
and we drove away. At the door of the
" Brindled Cow " a hamper was put into the
carriage, and whatever you may say of the
landlady she's a good sort, and I'll never
speak a word against her, though she wasn't
a favourite of mine. And all the children
came out of school, and waved their hands,
and cried, "God bless you, lady!" — Oh,
George, the world isn't so bad after all ;
there's plenty of good people in it, and we
met a many of them in Chudleigh village.
At last we got to the station, and at the very
moment the train was moving away, the door
of our carriage was quickly opened, and who
should jump into it but Chud! "Oh, my
dear, dear Chud," my dear mistress cried,
"you must go, you must go!" She tried to
push him out, but she might as well have
tried to move a mountain. There Chud lay
stretched out, with his great head between
his paws, licking my dear young lady's hands,
and he never stirred till the train was rattling

along. Then he got up, and put his head in her lap, and looked up into her face with his lovely speaking eyes, as much as to say, " I'm going to stop with you, and go where you go, and whoever tries to prevent me had better look out for himself." And they better had, for if ever a faithful heart beat in anyone's breast it beats in Chud's, and he'd lay down his life for his mistress, just as I would myself. She put her arms round him, and said, " Yes, Chud, if they don't take you away you shall remain with me, and we'll never, never part!" Chud gave me his paw, and we shook hands, if you don't mind my saying so, and here he is now in our room, blinking at me.

Well, George, we got to London all safe, and then we had to look out for lodgings. "We must find rooms among the poor, Rachel," my young lady said; and that is how we came to live here. We slept here last night for the first time, and before we went to bed I posted a letter to Mr. Palmer, and he came to see us to-day. What a gentleman he is—a real true gentleman—and

20*

how he comforted my young lady! He wants her to live nearer to him, and perhaps we shall after a week or so. The worst of it is, he's as poor as we are, but it's something to have such a friend in this great wilderness of a city. She wrote to her father this afternoon, and told him where she was, but I don't expect she'll get any answer from him.

And now, George, I've told you everything, and if anybody had said that I could write such letters as I've been doing lately I would never have believed him; but there's no knowing what you can do till you try. If you get this letter to-morrow, and care to come and see us, why, George, dear, we shall be glad to see you—at least, my young lady and Chud will; but if you're coming to scold me, and with any idea that you can make me alter my mind, you had better keep away. I'm longing to see you, George, and I know you will be good.

Your loving sweetheart,
RACHEL.

From the Rev. Mr. Burleigh, Gabriel's Gully, Otago, New Zealand, to G. Palmer, Esq., Westminster Palace Road, London.

MY DEAR SIR,—

You will be surprised to receive a letter from a stranger in a distant land, but I write to you, the father of a young friend I have made in these parts, for whom I have a sincere regard and esteem. I will at once allay any anxiety you may feel by saying that your son Frederick is well enough in health, and that there is nothing the matter with him physically; but I think it proper you should understand how it is with him in all ways.

You do not need to be told, dear sir, that you have for a son a gentleman of refined feeling and of honourable impulse. It is impossible for him to descend to a meanness; his is in every respect a noble character, which compels admiration from those who can understand him. But not everyone does this, lacking the qualification, and unluckily he is in a part of the world where the human atoms are not exactly of his order; therefore until he met me—you will pardon me for this piece of vanity — he was somewhat of a forlorn wanderer in these wilds, for wilds they are. Civilization approaches us, but we are as yet familiar with only its rougher attributes. In the course of time we shall do better. The restless, adventurous spirit brings out many noble qualities; it brings out, also, many of the baser. Unhappily, in the quest of gold, these latter predominate, and mortals commonly brought up, suddenly finding themselves in possession of gold, gravitate the wrong way,—and consequently fall. There is no fear of this with your son Frederick, and I have touched briefly upon the conditions of life among which we move, only for the purpose of enlightening you. If I judge aright your son would not disclose to you, his father, for whom he entertains an affection of which a father may be proud, the moral difficulties we adventurers from the old country have to contend with.

Your son wandered hitherward in search of gold, and he is out of place in the life we live. Success would have amply justified him; his want of success is a warning. I am myself of an age to be his father. My experience has been wide, and I have seen many lives wasted. It would cause me infinite regret to see your son's life wasted. I cannot disguise my apprehension that there is danger ahead. Men fall into an apathetic state; the more sensitive, the more refined the nature, the greater the danger. What is lacking is rough strength, and this is lacking in your son.

He has worked hard and has not been successful. He has seen other men achieve fortune, and it has passed him by. But he still clung to the mantle of hope. Lately, however, a change has come over him. Where he was hopeful he is becoming hopeless. Animation is degenerating into apathy. He works hard still, but the hope that sustained him is fading into listlessness. The light upon the hill is growing faint.

It hurts me to observe this. I ask myself the reason. He is young, he is talented, the best years of his life are before him. Let them not be wasted here, where there is small opportunity for him to work out a befitting career. He has told me much of himself, of you, of the lady he loves; but I am of the opinion that he has not told me all. A secret grief is preying upon him.

Let me, dear sir, advise you. Your son is not in his proper sphere amongst us. He has more than talent, he has genius. As an artist he may have to pass through years of struggle, but success will smile upon him at last. He will never meet with it here; all the elements of our outer and inner life are opposed to it and to him. His career should be worked out in a civilized land, where you are. He loves you; he has faith and confidence in you; if you can afford it, dear sir, send for him home. He will never win fortune here. Every day he remains is a day wasted.

If he had the means I would urge him to

take the first ship to England; but he has not the means. I doubt if he tells you how poor he is. He is working literally hand to mouth, and sometimes one does not reach the other. If I had the money I would force it upon him, but I am a poor minister, with a small stipend and a young family to devour it. That is the position exactly.

He is not aware that I am writing to you. I have obtained your address from him in a casual way, and he does not suspect my motive in asking for it. I am thoroughly disinterested in advising you to send for your son, for it will be a grievous loss to me, but I shall gain some compensation by an artful compact I intend to devise, that we shall correspond with each other, he giving me news of the old world, I giving him news of the new. In his career at home in the old land I shall take a genuine interest. His letters will be like a breath of sweet air from the familiar scenes of my youth. My wife and children have a very sincere affection for him, and will miss him as much as I shall

myself. Believe me, my dear sir, to remain,
with great respect,

Yours very truly,

HENRY M. BURLEIGH.

*From   G.   Palmer,   London,   to   Frederick
Palmer, New Zealand.*

MY DEAR BOY,—

I wrote to you three or four days
ago, and here I find myself suddenly writing
to you again.   There are two special reasons
for my taking up my pen again so soon.   One
springs from a circumstance in which I have
had no hand and taken no part ; but it is full
of significance for you and me.   The other
springs from my love for my dear lad.   You
may, if you please, call one fact and the other
fancy, but the latter, my heart tells me, is as
tangible as the former.   I will speak of the
fact first.

My dear Frederick, Agnes is in London,
driven from her father's home because she
refuses to marry a man whose suit he favours.
That this man is a scoundrel I have ample

proof, and notwithstanding that I am now upholding a charge against her parent, I commend and approve of Agnes' action in the matter. She has come ill provided with funds, and is accompanied by two faithful friends, a noble dog who shall sit to me for his picture, and the maid under whose care you have written to Agnes from New Zealand. She is therefore not without protectors. Her intention is to obtain some employment which will enable her to live until the necessity no longer devolves upon her. I do not seek to oppose this design ; it is admirable and praiseworthy, and I trust she will be able to carry it out. From what I have learned the breach between her and her father is not likely to be healed. Bound by her promise to him with respect to yourself she remains true to you, and will wed no other man. She is a sweet and patient lady, and I could wish my dear son no worthier wife, if it ever be your good fortune to be united to her. Until we meet, which I trust will be soon, you may depend that I shall look after her to the best of my ability. I will be a second father to her, kinder and tenderer hearted, I hope, than the father who has turned her from his doors. And this, my dear Frederick, brings me to my second reason for writing to you again so soon.

I dreamt of you last night. I saw you toiling on the goldfields, surrounded by uncongenial companions, living an unhappy life in an atmosphere which must be repugnant to you, deprived of love and all that makes life sweet. So mournful was your appearance in my dreams that I said, " Can this being, seemingly on the brink of despair, be the dear bright lad that has been the sunshine of my days? " My heart went out to you, my dear son, and so great was my trouble when I awoke that I took all your letters from New Zealand, and read them carefully through. Frederick, a light seemed to dawn upon me ; not till this morning have I read your letters aright. But now I read between the lines, and I see that you were concealing your unhappiness from me, and that there was something prophetic in my dreams. My dear lad, you have worked on the goldfields and have been unsuccessful, and I can see clearly—I am writing now with a prophetic mind—that you have less prospect of success there than ever. A large fortune is not needed for happiness; a modest competence will serve; and you have even here a brighter chance of gaining the former than where you are now so miserably toiling, away from home, and separated from all who are dear to you. Yes, Frederick, I not only read your letters again, I looked through your sketches and studied them by the new light. My dear lad, there is more promise in them than I ever discerned before; it is in your power to achieve great success, and you know what success as an artist means in England. It means fortune as well as fame—it means happiness—it means Agnes. When you have won distinction her father can no longer hold out. Come home, then, without delay, and work for your reward, come home and win it. My dear lad, I need you—my heart cries out for you ; Agnes needs you ; when she takes your hand in hers, brightness will come again into her eyes; your presence will lighten her heart. I implore you not to refuse. My heart tells me something more—that you have not the money to pay for your passage home. I enclose a draft that will defray all your expenses. We will work together, side by side, and all my early hopes will blossom into flower at my son's success. Surely I need say no more than I have already said. Make all you love happy by not losing a single day after the receipt of this letter. With heartfelt love,

I am, ever your affectionate father,

G. PALMER.

END OF VOL. II.